' "Here, Alan. You ___ carry one of these ___ effigy about three ___ A dozen of these we ___ . The biggest was m ___ it as well as the u ___ 'bodies' in a heap ___

Alan and Kathy unrolled their banner. It said in uneven, red capitals: WE DON'T WANT A NUCLEAR FUTURE.

"Poor execution, good message. Up it goes!" said Kathy.

With much laughter and joking, the fifty or so protesters got into a crocodile and started to walk towards Parliament Square . . .'

When the sleepy village of Stagwell is chosen as a possible nuclear-waste dump-site, Alan joins in enthusiastically with the fierce local protest campaign. After all, they've already got a nuclear power station and, as the news filters in about the Chernobyl disaster, Alan starts to wonder how safe it all really is. With Kathy, a girl at his school who is totally opposed to all forms of nuclear power, he throws all his energy into the campaign. But Kathy starts to feel impatient about the progress of the organized protest — she wants to see some more direct action . . .

Also by Peggy Woodford

PLEASE DON'T GO

published by Corgi Freeway Books

MONSTER IN OUR MIDST
PEGGY WOODFORD

CORGI
F·R·E·E·W·A·Y

MONSTER IN OUR MIDST

A CORGI FREEWAY BOOK   0 552 52491 3

Originally published in Great Britain
by Macmillan Children's Books

PRINTING HISTORY
Macmillan edition published 1988
Corgi Freeway edition published 1989

This book is set in 11/12pt Paladium.

Corgi Freeway Books are published by Transworld Publishers Ltd.,
61–63 Uxbridge Road, Ealing, London W5 5SA, in Australia by
Transworld Publishers (Australia) Pty. Ltd., 15–23 Helles
Avenue, Moorebank, NSW 2170, and in New Zealand by Transworld
Publishers (N.Z.) Ltd., Cnr. Moselle and Waipareira Avenues,
Henderson, Auckland.

Printed and bound in England by
Cox & Wyman Ltd., Reading, Berks.

MONSTER IN OUR MIDST

AUTHOR'S NOTE

All characters in this book are entirely imaginary, and bear no relation to anyone living or dead. With the exception of Chernobyl, the action and setting are also imaginary, although based closely upon real events. The experiences of people in Bedfordshire and Essex who protested against nuclear waste dumping have been particularly relevant.

The chapter headings dealing with the progress of the Chernobyl disaster are either based on reports in the national newspapers, or taken from the following sources:

The Worst Accident in the World, a book compiled by the scientific journalists on *The Observer*. (Pan Books 1986); copyright © *The Observer* Ltd 1986 reprinted by permission of William Heinemann Ltd.
Chernobyl UK, reproduced from a Greenpeace Report, 1987.
Sarcophagus, a play by Vladimir Gubaryev, translated by Michael Glenny (Penguin Plays, 1987), copyright © Vladimir Gubaryev, 1986, translation copyright © Michael Glenny, 1987.
Fear Itself, an article by Stephen Fried in *Philadelphia* Magazine, September 1986.

The Publishers gratefully acknowledge permission to reprint copyright material.

To my godson, Federico Gnoli

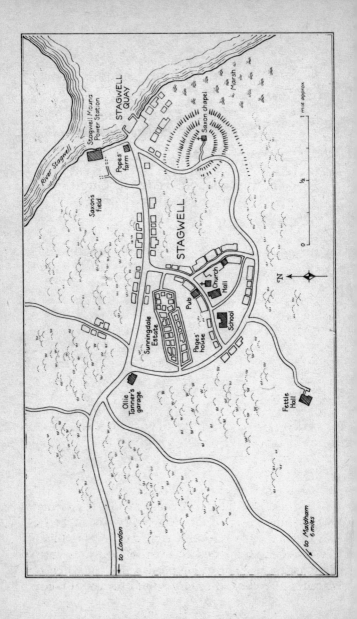

Nuclear power is the safest form of energy yet known to man.

PETER WALKER,
Britain's Energy Minister, 16 March 1986

ONE
Saturday, 26 April 1986

'Alan! Maddy!' Angie Page shouted up the stairs. 'Get up!'

Silence.

She shouted again, and eventually heard the distant waking-up groans of her son and daughter.

'I'm going out shopping with Luke, and while I'm out I want you to get up and start tidying and cleaning those disgusting rooms of yours. Today is blitz day.'

Silence.

'Do you hear me?'

'Yes, Mum.'

'They stink. Yours particularly, Alan. I'll be furious if you haven't got going before I get back.'

The front door slammed, its loose pane of glass rattling.

Alan, whose room was at the front, heard his little brother Luke say, 'I bet they don't get up,' while Angie was opening the car doors. Then the car coughed its way down the road. Alan stretched out; his feet hung over the end of the bed. A six-foot bed just wasn't big enough any more. He used a toe to switch on his radio. He looked briefly round his room before shutting his eyes again. The mess was worse than usual. Books, papers, files, games kit, dirty clothes, clean clothes, shoes, empty mugs, shrivelled apple cores, half-crushed Coke cans, a blackened banana skin. Even Alan found it all depressing.

The Pages were a chronically untidy family, and the only way Angie could cope with the ever-encroaching mess was to blitz it at regular intervals. Everyone would end up storming round the house in a bad temper until Angie was satisfied.

Before the divorce, blitzes never happened. Angie had kept the whole house clean and tidy; now that she worked all day as secretary of St George's Primary (Luke's school) she did not have the time. Besides, Alastair Page had been a tidiness freak, a real neatnik.

At the thought of his father, Alan got out of bed. He pulled the curtains and opened the window on a fine, still day. Birds sang in spring fever all round, almost drowning out the ever-present whine of the distant power station. Alan bounded down the narrow stairs, and proceeded to make his usual Saturday fry-up. Bacon, egg, fried bread (burnt), tomato. He propped up the sports page against the toaster and tucked in as he read.

Maddy lay in her tiny attic room gazing at the wooden ceiling, on to which she had pinned so many cuttings from magazines that she felt she slept under a tent of beautiful faces, hair, bodies, arms, legs. Just above her, her favourite model did a row of somersaults along a sandy beach, empty sea and sky behind her. There were six photographs showing different stages of the somersault, and a seventh of the girl on tiptoe, arms high, her breasts bare and her bikini bottom covered with sand. Maddy stared at this lithe perfect body, and felt herself grow lither and slimmer and taller. She closed her eyes, unwilling to get up and see the reality of her reflection in her long mirror: white stubby legs, not fat but too short; too much flesh round her stomach and not enough round her breasts; freckled arms and face, horrible headful of ginger curly hair. Why, oh why, oh why, had she been the only one to inherit her father's colouring, on top of everything else? Why wasn't she dark and petite like Angie, or dark and tall like Alan? Even Luke with his auburn hair had had a better deal than her. Except for her eyes, which were large and bright blue, she'd trade the lot in any day.

She heard Alan go downstairs, but did not join him. She had a blitz on the house looming, and there was a maths test on Monday. Great weekend.

Towards evening, the blitz over, Alan and Maddy were sitting in Alan's room revising for their exams. Since their birthdays occurred in the same academic year — Alan was born in September and Maddy eleven months later — they were in the same class at school. The comprehensive for Stagwell was in the nearest big town, Maldham. Despite people's worries that being in the same class could have a bad effect on one or the other, Alan and Maddy found it an advantage. They could share textbooks at home; they could test each other and revise at the same time; they could moan about the same teachers. Maddy's strong subjects were different from Alan's: she was good at physics and chemistry, and history. Alan shone at art, English and French. Maddy was slightly better at maths, Alan at biology.

'I've had enough maths. Test me on some French. Those awful reflexive verbs.' Maddy got up and stretched, looking out of the window as she did so. She saw her mother going across the road to the house

11

opposite. 'Mum's gone over to the Norringtons' again. I'm glad she's made some new friends.'

'Do you know what Paul Norrington does?'

'No.'

'He's the assistant manager of the power station.'

'Really? Does Mum know?'

'Mum told me.'

They stared across at Paul Norrington, who was showing Angie some plant in the front garden.

'He's quite good-looking in a wimpish sort of way,' said Maddy. 'I think Mum quite fancies him.'

'Come on, Maddy, if you want me to test you. I want to fix up my evening soon.'

An hour or so later, Luke came in. 'I'm hungry. Where's Mum?'

'Opposite, at the Norringtons'. Go and get her,' Maddy told him.

'No, you go.'

'You go.'

Luke fidgeted round the room, ignored by the others. He was small for ten, and thin; he had to wear glasses, which he hated and frequently lost or broke. The current pair were heavily mended with Sellotape. 'Let's go and do the cooking ourselves, then. There's chicken in the kitchen. I chose chicken for tonight.'

'Big surprise. You never choose anything else.'

'Come on, Maddy, let's stop work now. I'm hungry, too,' said Alan.

The three of them went down and prepared the food. The chicken pieces were put in the oven, the potatoes scrubbed and put in, too; the cabbage was chopped. Ever since their father had left, the shopping and cooking had become much more of a family activity. All three knew how much their mother depended on their help.

'Why doesn't Mum come back?' whined Luke when the smells from the kitchen announced that the food was nearly ready. 'I'm ravenous.'

'No idea. Perhaps she's having a good time.' Alan half-watched the telly while he sketched aimlessly on a pad. 'Go and tell her the food won't be long.'

'You go.'

'You're the hungry one.'

'You said you were hungry, too.'

'I'm not on the point of collapse like you.'

Luke suddenly left the window where he had been hovering. 'She's coming right now.'

The front door opened noisily, and Angie rushed in, her face very flushed. Her eyes sparkled. 'Oh, kids, I am sorry. I had no idea how late it was. I've been having a drink with the Norringtons.' She crashed around the kitchen, and opened the oven door. 'The chicken looks lovely. Those potatoes need longer, though.' She straightened up and pushed her hair off her face. 'Goodness, I feel hot.' She caught Alan's eye and grinned sheepishly. 'Yes, I know my face is red. I shouldn't have had that last glass of wine. Then Paul and Elaine asked me to go out for a curry with them, and I realised I hadn't given a thought to your meal.'

'Since it's all done, why don't you go out with them?' Maddy said in a rather taut voice without looking at her mother.

'Well . . .'

'I'll eat your chicken piece,' said Luke. 'I could eat three.'

Angie put her hand on Maddy's arm. 'Would you mind if I went out, then? I'd love a curry, I must say. They're going to that new place in Maldham.'

'Go, Mum, go.' Maddy moved away from her mother.

Angie looked at Alan. 'You won't go out and leave Luke on his own, will you?'

'Stop fussing, Mum. I'm not going out anyway,' said Maddy. 'Little Lukey-Wukey will be okey-dokey—'

'Shut up.' Luke leapt at her with teeth bared. Alan put out an arm and blocked his path. Angie went out humming, and tripped over the front mat.

'Mum's pissed,' said Alan as the front door shut.

After eating, Alan did some telephoning and discovered all his friends were tied up. Usually a group of them went to Maldham on a Saturday night; if funds allowed, they ended up in a club. But tonight, for a mixture of boring reasons, no one could come out. Even Nick Pope, Alan's best friend, was stuck; he had to stay in and babysit, and invited Alan to come over. Alan left it open, but decided after several more fruitless calls that going over to Nick's was infinitely preferable to staying at home while Maddy and Luke bickered.

He got his bike out and set off. Nick lived down at Stagwell Quay, ten minutes away. Stagwell was really two villages: Stagwell itself with its old church of St George's, and the Quay situated down on the estuary. If the houses continued to spread down the road Alan was bicycling along, Stagwell would soon be all one small town.

He cycled past the church with its stocks and cluttered graveyard. He drew level with the pub and peered in through the small-paned windows. The George and Dragon was full tonight, but he saw no one he particularly wanted to talk to so he continued down the road. He was broke anyway. He was always broke.

There were two roads to Stagwell Quay: the more direct one which took the traffic to the power

14

station, and one which climbed a small hill where there was a Saxon chapel and then provided a steep downhill run. Alan preferred this way, though it took longer. It was always deserted, and he liked having the road to himself.

Eeeeeeeeeeeeeeeeee. . . . Tonight that sound got to him. Day and night, year in year out, the power station's high-pitched whine filled every Stagwell ear. The process of nuclear fission powering circulators and turbines made a noise that travelled clearly over a three-mile radius. *Eeeeeeeeee.* The sound was like a combination of a mosquito and the whine of cars on a distant motorway, and it bit insidiously into thousands of brains.

Tonight Alan was particularly conscious of it. He was tired after a week of hard work, and in a bad mood because Saturday night had turned boring. When he reached the top of the hill where the ancient chapel stood, he stopped for a moment. On his right was the squat dark building, simple as a child's drawing, built over a thousand years ago. Below was Stagwell Quay, with its village, its marina and little harbour along the edge of the estuary. The tide was high, and water shone in the moonlight. Also shining in the moonlight was the power station. It sat on a little promontory known as Stagwell Mound, but whatever shape the mound had had was now flattened by the weight of two twentieth-century gas-cooled Magnox reactors, both encased in steel and concrete to make everyone feel safe and sound. Alan gazed at the grey and silver planes of the station, and saw benign industrial shapes. An owl hooted nearby, audible above the nuclear whine. Safe and sound. The only person he knew who queried this was Mr Hawkes, his physics master, but then he was a bit of a nutter about things nuclear, and a member

15

of Greenpeace as well. Yet to have your own physics master so anti-nuclear was a bit worrying.

'Nick Pope, you live nearest the power station. Tell the class what you feel about it.'

'I forget it's there half the time,' said Nick.

'Do you never think about a Three Mile Island-type disaster? Widespread contamination?'

'The Americans have cleaned it all up, though, haven't they, Mr Hawkes?' said Alan.

'Not so. Listen to this. The disaster was seven years ago, in 1979; they've been trying to clean up ever since. But as soon as they've scrubbed the concrete buildings clean they promptly recontaminate themselves from the inside. And they're finding it just as difficult to decontaminate the ground.'

'You mean, if there was an accident here at Stagwell, we'd have to leave our farm permanently?'

'Too right.'

Alan thought about this recent conversation with Mr Hawkes. He could see Nick's house from where he was, on the edge of Stagwell Quay close to the power station. The yard was full of Ken Pope's farm machinery, much of it broken and out of use but still left in the corners of the yard. Alan could see the kitchen light was on, and another light upstairs which went out at that moment. Nick had obviously got his little sister off to bed. Alan whizzed down the final slope into Stagwell Quay, his feet on the handlebars. Nick lived on the far side, past the marina; a strong smell of sea-water and mud-flats came from the estuary. Bits of tin tied to marker-buoys tinkled incessantly, sounding like a flock of goats on a hillside. The whine of the power station was loud now; it was less than a mile away. As Alan cycled past the neatly lined-up boats in the marina, he looked through their rocking masts at its great bulk. A

16

huge sleeping dragon with a sting in its tail. Safe and sound. . . . It had better be.

Nick found the sloe gin hidden behind the breadbin in the larder.

'Look, we'll just have a bit each, and top the bottle up with Michelle's Ribena.' He poured an inch into two teacups. 'They'll never know. They got a bit annoyed last time.'

'We had even less than this each.'

'Yes, but there were seven of us.'

Nick and Alan settled down into a decrepit old sofa in the corner of the untidy but large kitchen. The television sat on a packing-case. Nick put his feet on this and turned the set off with his foot. 'Just rubbish on tonight. Have some crisps.'

As they munched through a packet, Alan said: 'I don't know why, but I was thinking about Three Mile Island tonight.'

'I wish Hawkes would shut up about it. It gives me nightmares.'

Alan lay back. 'We'd just come to Stagwell. I didn't know you then except as a name at school.'

'I'd forgotten you came then.'

'Dad had just bought our first house, and of course he didn't think twice about the nuclear station nearby. Then *boom*! Three Mile Island starts blowing up.' Alan shut his eyes. 'I can see my dad now, shouting and yelling at Mum.'

Alan remembered his father's angry voice and his mother's misery. *I wish I hadn't bought this damned house! It's all your fault; you were so keen on it! We paid too bloody much — it's a financial disaster!* This scene was played out again and again with variations until the American crisis had blown over and Stagwell had returned to normal.

17

'Then of course Dad went round saying an accident like that couldn't happen here, because he'd been over the power station. I think all the locals were invited to view it and have a reassuring chat—'

'My dad refused to go. He said he didn't want to be brainwashed.'

They sipped their sloe gin and sat in silence for a while. Alan knew that it was during all those rows and arguments that his parents' marriage finally fell apart. They weren't friends any more. The air was poisoned by their bickering; rows never came to a head as they had in the old days. Each day had started with an increasing backlog of unhappiness.

'I'll tell you something I haven't told anyone. I was glad, actually glad, when my father left us. I couldn't stand the atmosphere in the house another day. I couldn't talk to Mum about it. I tried to talk to Maddy, but she couldn't face it. She was really close to Dad. She couldn't handle it at all when she realised he'd gone off for ever.'

'She must have been the same age as Michelle now — eight.'

As if summoned by her name, Michelle appeared at the kitchen door.

'Go back to bed.'

'I need a drink of milk.'

'Well, hurry up.'

'Can I have some crisps?'

'No.'

'You're a meanie.'

'There aren't any left anyway.'

'I saw some packets hidden in that drawer.'

'If Mum's hidden them there, it means she doesn't want you to get them.' Nick pushed the cup of sloe gin out of sight. Michelle was eventually persuaded back to bed.

'Did your dad just have a final big row and leave one day or what?'

'No, he went on a business trip and never came back. He moved in with his secretary instead. He only stayed with her for a few months before he chucked her, too. Mind you, we knew it wouldn't last. Her name didn't begin with an A.'

'You're joking.'

'Only partly. My dad's fixated on this name business. All Pages marry people with names beginning with A. It's crazy.'

'What was the secretary called?'

'Fanny.' Delighted grins spread over the boys' faces. 'I'm not kidding. She really was called Fanny. The rumour was they split up because she wouldn't change her name to something Dad wanted, like Alice or Amanda.'

'People really are crazy.'

'So Dad went to Australia, and we haven't seen him since. He writes to us occasionally. He's making a packet out there, or so he says. Good luck to him. I don't care if I never see the bastard again.' Alan was digging his thumbnail viciously into the sofa, and some stuffing oozed out. 'God, I've made a hole.'

'Don't worry. We all give that sofa a hard time.'

'What I'm really dreading is for Mum to marry again. It's unthinkable. Just imagine some creep moving in and causing us grief. I'd leave home.'

'Who's her boyfriend?'

'She hasn't got one. She never goes out. Well, hardly ever.'

'Then, relax,' said Nick, rolling the crisp-packet into a ball and throwing it for the cat to play with. 'It may never happen.'

In the accident at Three Mile Island in March 1979 two-thirds of the fuel disintegrated, with eleven tons melting and slumping to the bottom of the reactor pressure vessel. That accident was brought about by a series of small, unrelated events which individually were accidents within the design plan but when compounded led to an 'incredible' event. A good measure of luck prevented the TMI accident from developing into a disaster on a scale equal to Chernobyl.

Greenpeace Report, 1987

TWO
Monday, 29 April

was not a day anyone in Stagwell was likely to forget. On the morning of that day, Stagwell was informed that it was being considered as a possible dump-site for nuclear waste. Inhabitants were assured that no danger would result from this dump: stringent measures would be taken to make sure no radioactive waste could escape. Etc. Etc.

When Angie came home at four o'clock with Luke she found Alan and Maddy in the kitchen eating bread and peanut butter.

'You're back early.'

'No games today.'

'I wish you'd use plates instead of putting your bread straight on the table. Peanut butter is everywhere.'

'We'll clear it up.' Maddy started cutting Luke some bread.

'By the way, the whole village is buzzing. We've just learnt that the Government has chosen Stagwell as a nuclear-waste dump-site.'

'You're joking.' Alan's bread got only halfway to his mouth.

'I am not. It was officially announced this morning.'

'As if having a nuclear power station isn't enough. . . .'

'Perhaps that's why they chose us,' said Maddy. 'We've got used to the idea of radioactivity.'

'There's going to be trouble over this.' Alan finally ate his bread. 'Mr Hawkes will do his nut.'

'He's a nutcase anyway.'

'Oh, very funny.'

'I wish he'd stick to his job and teach us physics instead of ranting on about the dangers of nuclear power—'

'It's people like him who'll save us in the end.'

'What nonsense you're talking, Alan,' said Angie. 'I agree with Maddy. I think Mr Hawkes is an alarmist who does more harm than good.'

The phone rang. Alan reached out and took the receiver off the wall phone above the kitchen table. Nick's voice said: 'Hi. You won't believe this — we're going to have a lovely nuclear dump just beside our farm. Aren't we lucky?'

'Mum just told me the good news.'

'Dad is so furious he's decided to form a protest group, and he's gone off to see Mark Ableman who apparently organised an anti-nuclear protest in the States.'

'He's moved fast.'

'I've never seen him so mad. Really mad. He said twenty-five years ago he and Grandad voted against the bloody power station and lost, and now we've

21

been landed with a new threat we're not going to lose this time. He'll raise the roof.'

Ken Pope was a large noisy man whose voice could be heard across a ten-acre field. He had huge red hands and the widest shoulders Alan had ever seen. Once, a few years back, Alan had noticed his blue denim boiler-suit pegged out in the Popes' back garden, and had stared at it in wonder. He and Nick were able both to get inside it, taking a leg each, and there was still room over.

The phone rang several times in the next hour; the conversations were all of the have-you-heard and what-shall-we-do variety. Then at five past six Nick rang again.

'Are you watching the six o'clock news? Go and watch it. There's been a nuclear accident in Russia. No one knows how big, but the Swedes are being doused with radiation.'

Alan rushed to the television and switched channels, taking no notice of Luke's anguished cry.

'An American safety expert has said the Russian accident makes Three Mile Island look like a tea party. The leak is so large that it has prompted a full-scale alert nearly a thousand miles away in Sweden. . . .'

Alan watched and listened in frozen horror. Suddenly Sweden didn't seem that far away.

Huge Nuclear Leak at Soviet Plant. Moscow Admits Casualties. Radiation Spreads Across Europe.

Alan stared down at the newspaper lying on the doormat next morning. At last he picked it up and took it into the kitchen where he handed it silently to Angie. She looked at the headlines and then put the paper aside.

'What's going to happen to us here?' asked Alan at last.

22

'Nothing.' She pointed to another headline. *Britain Safe*. '*Britain has no need to fear radiation released at Chernobyl*. . . . Have your breakfast and don't worry about it. There's nothing we can do.'

'They'd say there was nothing to worry about even if there was. . . .'

'I've done you two slices of bacon.'

'Aren't you worried?'

'Paul Norrington says there's nothing to worry about, and I believe him. Get on with your food, love, or you'll miss the bus.'

By Thursday, 1 May, Alan was beginning to feel very confused. Newspapers contained conflicting statistics of two dead, of 300 dead, of 2,000 dead; nobody even seemed to know if the reactor core was melting. The only clear information was that the station was still belching smoke and radioactivity, that an eighteen-mile radius had been evacuated of people, and that the crisis was still a crisis.

Alan had arranged that first day of May to meet Nick for an hour's fishing before school. He biked down to Stagwell Quay at six-thirty; the sky was cloudless and pale blue, and the towns and beaches on the other side of the estuary were crystal clear. So was the power station. Its silver sides gleamed, washed down by all the recent rain.

Nick was already preparing the Popes' battered old dinghy, and the two boys dragged it down into the water. Nick rowed, while Alan put the lines out. The power station was very close to them; the whine seemed to bounce over the water. Between them was the barrier wall which was built in the estuary near the station to house the pumps which sucked up thousands of gallons of sea-water a day to cool the condensers. Grey mullet were also sucked out of

23

the sea and floundered about in the culverts until they died.

'You have to believe it's safe or you'd go mad,' said Nick. 'The experts are all saying an accident like Chernobyl couldn't happen here because our safety standards are better. I heard one of them say you'd be as likely to get an explosion in a currant bun as in one of our power stations.'

'They're arseholes, those nuclear energy chiefs. They're so full of confidence it makes you sick. They use words like "impossible", but we all know what that could mean. A few human errors and *wham*! Think of Ed Mallory being anywhere near a crucial button.'

'God. It doesn't bear thinking about.'

Ed Mallory worked at the reactor, but before that he had been one of Ken Pope's farmhands. He had been useless, with a genius for causing muddles. When he knocked a wooden shed down with a tractor by mistake, Ken fired him.

Alan lay back and stared at the sky. Nick shipped the oars and lay back, too. The sun was getting stronger, the sky bluer; the waves slapped and danced around them. He pulled a packet from under one of the thwarts and unwrapped two bacon sandwiches. 'Mum made them for us last night.' They bit hungrily into them. When he'd finished, Nick said: 'I feel deeply tempted to take the day off.'

They looked at each other. 'We could row across to Frampton and spend the day there.' Alan shut his eyes. 'Let's go.'

'OK. Let's go.'

'Great.'

Alan stretched and basked in the sun. Then Nick said: 'I haven't got any money. Have you?'

'No.'

'And we've just eaten all our food.'

'Ah, well, another time.'

'Another time.'

They caught a couple of grey mullet, and then realised it was time to get back. Nick whistled happily, while Alan rowed; he said as they beached the boat: 'I still think it's a crime to spend a day like this indoors. See you on the bus.'

Alan picked the newspaper off the mat as he entered his house. *Chernobyl — Second Reactor Threatened*, he read. And: *Radiation fears put even May Day under a cloud*.

'It's just a gigantic kettle. All reactors in all nuclear power stations are essentially the same. They use the heat generated when atoms of uranium are split to boil water, which produces steam to turn electrical turbines.' Mr Hawkes pointed to the simple diagram he had drawn. 'The underlying process in a reactor is simple. Uranium is first placed inside long metal canisters, and these are then slotted into the graphite core of the reactor. This graphite core acts as a moderator — in other words it slows down the neutrons that are emitted by the disintegrating uranium atoms. They have to be slowed down because they usually fly out at speeds which are too fast for interaction with other uranium atoms. No interaction, no nuclear fission. So they have to be moderated by graphite. But, before I go on, someone define fission for me.'

There was the usual silence.

'Sally Dews, define fission.'

'Er. Um. Atoms breaking up, like. . . .' Sally tailed off.

'Maddy?'

'Well, it's the process when certain very unstable

25

atoms can be made to break up . . . er, to break up in a runaway fashion.'

'Yes, yes, go on. What is meant by "runaway fashion"?'

Maddy ignored the giggles and remarks about jogging-suits. 'Say you have a uranium atom split apart by a neutron. From the remains smaller atoms are formed, energy is released, etc. But so are more neutrons, and these strike other atoms, they split apart and even more energy is released. So it goes on. Runaway.'

'Very good, Maddy. Sally, I hope you followed all that.' Sally nodded, knowing she could copy Maddy's notes later. 'And now perhaps you could tell us when the first self-sustaining nuclear fission was produced?'

'Me, sir?'

'You, Sally.'

Sally went red, and mumbled: 'I don't know, sir.'

'It is in your notes.'

'Nineteen forty-two,' came from various directions.

Mr Hawkes kept his gaze on Sally. 'Can you redeem yourself by telling us how much coal would have to be used in a conventional power station to produce the energy one kilogram of uranium gives in a reactor?'

'I haven't learnt those notes yet, sir.' She had tears in her eyes.

'Well, I should stop crying and learn them or you won't enjoy your exams very much. Somebody else tell me.'

'Three thousand tonnes, sir.'

'Right. So no wonder man saw advantages in nuclear fission.' Hawkes turned back to his diagram. 'Back to the gigantic kettle. So, here is the graphite core. Into it are slotted control rods; fission cannot take place when they are inside the core. But when they are slowly removed, fission begins and heat is produced. By moving these rods in and out of the reactor, operators control the neutron flow and the heat production. If the rods become damaged or buckled, or are all taken out, you get meltdown. Something of that kind has just happened at Chernobyl. And if the burning core should by any chance be forced through the earth's crust, then the whole water-table would be contaminated for possibly hundreds of years. That is what is elegantly known as the "worst-case scenario".' The class went silent.

'Could that happen here?'

'It could happen anywhere. And one day, somewhere, it undoubtedly will.'

'But they keep saying nothing like that could happen in England, because our safety standards are so good.'

'Let's hope they're right. Now, we've got two minutes left and I want to use them for something special. There's been some talk in Russia about the meaning of the word *chernobyl*. By a strange coincidence, it means "wormwood". Now, what is wormwood, you may well ask. Well, it's a tree whose wood has an extremely bitter taste. Wormwood became the symbol for all that is painful and bitter to the soul.'

The whole class stared fixedly at him. He took a piece of paper from a folder and began to read what was copied on it.

' "The third angel blew his trumpet; and a great star shot from the sky, flaming like a torch; and it fell on a third of the rivers and springs. The name of the star was Wormwood; and a third of the water turned to wormwood, and men in great numbers died of the water because it had been poisoned." '

There was another silence. Alan felt his skin

27

crawling and asked Mr Hawkes where the words had come from.

'From the Book of Revelation at the end of the Bible. It's a sort of prophecy about the end of the world. That's where it comes from.'

Alan sat beside Maddy on the school bus because he knew Nick was staying on in Maldham. Also, Maddy was eating a bag of chips, and he was hungry.

'Hands off. Go and get some of your own.'

'Lend me the money, then.'

'I haven't got any cash left.'

'I'm starving.'

'Go on, then.' Resignedly, Maddy opened her bag of chips, and Alan took a clutch. 'I didn't say have the lot.' Maddy speeded up her rate of consumption.

'That was weird, that piece about wormwood and Chernobyl,' said Alan.

'I wish Mr Hawkes would stick to physics. We've got an exam in a few weeks. If he wants to read us the Bible, he ought to switch to teaching RE. I'm getting fed up with him.'

Alan licked the vinegar and salt off his fingers without replying. The driver got into the coach and started the engine. Three more minutes for latecomers to arrive. Then Alan noticed a girl pushing a moped towards the coach, while balancing a large flat box on the seat. She was having problems, and suddenly she put the bike on its stand and rushed over to the coach with the parcel. She got inside and stood beside the driver, searching for someone. She had wild black hair and green eyes; her expression was sharp, alert, satirical. Alan couldn't take his eyes off her.

'Janice!' She called Janice Wilson, who was keeping out of sight behind Alan. 'Take this home for me, would you? I can't manage it on the bike.'

28

'What is it?'

'None of your business.'

'I'm not taking it for you unless you tell me.'

The girl had come down the aisle and was standing beside Alan; the parcel she was holding clearly weighed a lot. It dug into his shoulder.

'Sorry.'

'Give it here. I'll put it on the rack.' Alan squeezed out beside her, and between them they stowed the heavy object away. Alan was surprised at the girl's strength.

'Thanks.' The girl grinned at him and pushed past him to get out.

'Go on, Kathy, what is it?'

'A synthesizer.'

'You didn't buy it off that slob Harry Hampton?'

'Why not? I beat him down. See you at the bus stop the other end.' Kathy leapt off the coach and ran to her moped. She pulled her helmet over her face; all that remained visible were her bright mocking eyes. She started the bike with a practised kick and drove off in a sharp turn.

'Kathy who?' Alan asked Maddy.

'Kathy Wilson.'

'I didn't know Janice Wilson had a sister.'

'She keeps it well hidden. Kathy's trouble.'

FALL-OUT FROM CHERNOBYL OVER BRITAIN
The first signs of radiation were detected in the south
east, but concentrates of radioactivity are too low to
be a danger to health.

The cloud contains 3 chemicals, caesium, iodine
and ruthenium. Caesium is the most deadly; it is highly
radioactive, incorporates itself in tissue and takes
30 years to deteriorate. . . .

The Daily Telegraph

THREE
Saturday, 3 May

Maddy was late leaving — Sally expected her ten
minutes ago. She grabbed a piece of bread and
drank a glass of milk; she was finishing this as Alan
came in.

'Drinka Pinta Iodine-131 a Day.' Alan poured
himself some orange juice.

'What?'

'You could get cancer of the thyroid.'

Maddy looked in horror at the cloudy white film
in her empty milk-glass.

'Don't flap. That milk's a few days old. It couldn't
possibly be contaminated.'

'You didn't have to scare me.'

'Sorry. But the whole business is scary, Maddy.
You don't seem to take that in.'

'I think everyone's exaggerating. Chernobyl,
Chernobyl, Chernobyl. It's miles away, and the

experts say there's no danger to us.' She pointed to the headline.

'Bollocks. Nobody really knows what a safe level of radiation actually is. There's a cloud of radiation over us right here in Stagwell, at this very moment. So what do we do? The air outside feels and looks just the same as usual. If radioactivity was blue, we could tell at a glance how strong it was. Instead we have to believe what we read in the papers, and trust the politicians and bureaucrats who don't know their arse from their elbow.'

'What do you mean, what do we do?' Maddy gave a worried look at the clock.

'Well, you're protected from direct radiation if you stay inside a building. Mr Hawkes says dozens of Russian kids are going to die eventually from the fact that they were allowed to play outside straight after the disaster. So what should we do if there's a cloud of radiation over Essex? We stay inside until it goes away.'

'Stay inside? You're mad. No one's told us to do that.'

'No one told the Russians, either.'

'Anyway, Sally and I are going into Maldham. I'm having my hair cut today.' Maddy fiddled with her springy ginger hair, which she corralled into a rubber band at the nape of her neck. 'I've been steeling myself to have it cut for weeks and I'm not stopping now.'

'It's your life.'

'If radiation doesn't get me, something else will. What's the point in worrying?'

'No point. Are you having your hair cut really short this time?'

'That's why Sally is coming with me. She knows I'd end up having a trim yet again because I'm too much of a coward to take the plunge. I must rush. Tell Mum I'll be back for tea.'

Maddy paused again at the door. 'Are you staying inside all day, then?'

'No. I've got a tennis match this afternoon, so I haven't much choice.'

'So what's the point of fussing?'

'I'm not fussing. I was just trying to make people aware of the fact that nobody in England has a clue what to do in the face of nuclear catastrophe. It's a case of the blind leading the blind.'

The doorbell rang; as Maddy left, she let Nick in. 'Watch out, Nick, he's heavily into Nuke Puke.'

'Ha ha.' Alan pushed her through the front door.

'What did she say?' Nick looked puzzled.

'Maddy's decided to stick her head in the sand.'

'Are you coming to the meeting tonight?'

'What meeting?'

'Anti the nuclear-waste dump. Dad and Mark Ableman have got it organised — they've stuck notices up inviting anyone who's interested to come along. Dad says I've got to go and bring along some friends — he wants some young faces, he says.'

'He'll be lucky. It's a Saturday night.'

'Look, I've got to go. I can't get out of it. Dad says it'll be over by nine. Come, Alan; I'll need moral support. Then we can go out afterwards. I couldn't face the meeting on my own. Dad is bound to kill me with embarrassment.'

'OK. My match should be over by six. Where's the meeting?'

'At St George's Hall at seven-thirty. I'll come and get you. I'm not going near the place on my own. I don't trust Dad an inch.'

It was turning into a weekend of doing boring things,

thought Alan as he went up to his room. His mother had warned him that the whole family were invited to Sunday lunch at the Norringtons'.

'Why?'

'What do you mean, *why*? Why shouldn't people be friendly to neighbours?'

'Do we have to come?'

'Yes.'

'You go on your own; they don't really want us.'

'Alan, don't be silly. Some people actually like talking to their friends' children, particularly if talking to young people isn't something they do every day.'

'They'll regret it. People always do. You can see their smiles growing strained when they get too near teenagers. Just take Luke with you. At least he'll eat lots of food.'

'You've all got to come, and that's it. Elaine's probably got the whole meal planned and organised by now. She's that sort of person. Please, Alan, don't be difficult. You need only stay for an hour or so. It's not often we get invited out to a meal, after all. The combination of single mother and three kids seems to put most people off.' Angie's voice was bitter. Alan couldn't think why she minded. Going out for meals in other people's houses was not a pastime he enjoyed. He always seemed to grow an extra pair of elbows, and his hands kept dropping things.

But he was pleased with his elbows and hands that afternoon. He had played well in the match, and his backhand had improved over the winter even though he hadn't played for several months. He could feel the strength going down his arm into the racket as he pasted the balls into awkward corners of the court. His team was playing the junior team of the Maldham Tennis Club, an up-market club which occasionally bred a Wimbledon player. They were up-market

33

socially, too, definitely the 'OK. Ya' brigade. But Alan liked his opposite captain, Guy Winter, despite the fact that Guy arrived at the match in his new car and lived at Fettle Hall, a large house just outside Stagwell.

'Well done. That was a really good match,' said Guy when Alan's team, surprisingly, won. He was always generous with praise, while his team tended to melt away, talking only to each other. 'You must come over and play a game at Fettle. I'm always trying to find someone good to play against. Lift home?'

'I'm on my bike, thanks.'

'You must be knackered already, and it's five miles at least to Stagwell. Come on, I can put the bike in the back of my car.'

Alan noticed it was well after six o'clock and he'd be pushed for time. 'Thanks, that would be great.'

Guy swung Alan's bike into the open Golf boot with a fine disregard for shiny paintwork. The boot wouldn't shut properly, so they tied it down with a sock and set off. About halfway home the sock came off and the boot swung upwards.

'Blast.' Guy stopped the car; it happened to be the highest part of the road, from where one could see the whole estuary. Stagwell and its power station lay below them, pinkish in the setting sun. The gabled roofs of Fettle Hall were visible, too, with rooks wheeling in the trees surrounding it. On the estuary, a magnificent red-sailed boat was slowly moving out to sea. Both boys stared at it in silence before getting back into the car.

'Are you going to the meeting tonight?' said Guy suddenly.

Alan was so surprised that Guy even knew about it that he didn't answer immediately. Guy went on: 'Ken Pope — you know, one of my father's tenant

34

farmers — is organising it. He's trying to get everyone who cares about the land to go.'

'I know about it. Nick Pope is a good friend of mine. Are you going?'

'My father certainly is. I'm a bit tied up myself. . . .' Guy's voice trailed off. The twin reactors were now bright as the sun descended into reddish cloud. The red-sailed ketch disappeared behind them. 'Beautiful boat, that,' said Guy. 'I've seen it before. Wonder who it belongs to. Wouldn't mind one like that myself.'

When Alan and Nick arrived at St George's Hall, it was already full. They stood at the back, propping themselves against an unsteady table which gave hints it might collapse if sat upon. On the small stage were Ken Pope, Robin Hawkes, a woman called Pam Webb who ran the local minicab service, and the Reverend Mark Ableman, an American who had exchanged parishes with Stagwell's vicar for a six-month period.

Alan looked round the crowd. He saw Guy with his father, Sir Oliver. Guy's old anorak did not quite conceal the fact that he was wearing a dinner-jacket and bow-tie underneath. He waved at Alan and, after a word with his father, came to the back.

'Can I join you? I've got to leave at eight, so it would be sensible to be at the back.' He noticed Nick's eyes flicking uneasily over his clothes, and added: 'Sorry about the get-up.' Nick shrugged; he didn't have much time for Guy. Once, when they were small boys, he had been asked to Guy's birthday party at the Hall, and been sick on the croquet lawn after tea, just by a hoop.

Ken Pope's loud voice rose above the hubbub. 'Shall we have a bit of hush, ladies and gents? We want to start the meeting.' Silence fell; Ken stood there beaming. He was looking unusually tidy in a vast tweed jacket, a white shirt and even a tie. Nick had rarely known his father make such an effort.

'Twenty-five years ago we had a meeting in this hall to decide whether we wanted the power station. Eighty people came. Only seventeen voted against.' He stared round the now silent hall. 'We were so green in those days. There was no protest, no worries about radiation. Today we all feel differently. We wouldn't be here tonight if we weren't worried. *We do not like* the Government's proposal to use Stagwell as a nuclear-waste dump. The buggers can find somewhere else to put their muck!'

There was a roar of laughter, with clapping and shouting. Nick buried his face in his collar and closed his eyes. No one could have a more embarrassing father; it was almost as bad as the front-page photo of Ken in the *Maldham Echo* standing pointing at the signs he had put up round his fields: 'Danger! Trespassers will become radioactive!'

Robin Hawkes started speaking in his quietly persuasive voice. 'We're here to plan what to do. I got in touch with Bedfordshire County Council because I knew they had organised a very effective campaign against Nirex. Nirex, by the way, stands for Nuclear Industry Radioactive Waste Executive.' He pointed to the walls. 'Those posters were sent me by the Bedfordshire group; I think they're very eye-catching. That's the sort of thing we ought to produce ourselves.'

The two posters nearest Alan and Nick were particularly good. One used the nuclear logo of three black wedge-shapes round a central black circle and made it the face of a skull and crossbones. The four shapes evilly suggested eyes, nose and mouth. The other poster showed a photo taken from above of at least a hundred schoolchildren standing together in a playground to form the word NO. 'No to Nirex.' Some of the kids were breaking ranks and raising their arms in excitement — the NO was on the point of dissolving.

'They've also brought out a good information leaflet about types of radioactive-waste dumps. I suggest we buy some of theirs for our own use.'

Up stood Ken. 'What are we going to use for money? This has all got to be set up properly, with a chairman, committee, treasurer, and all members paying a sub. Then we can talk of buying leaflets.'

Alan, Nick and Guy talked in undertones to each other while the committee was formed. Then a chairman had to be elected. Ken Pope's name was shouted from various corners. Nick turned to Alan and said: 'They're crazy if they elect Dad. Let's go. I can't stand this any longer.'

'No, hang on, Nick.' Both Alan and Guy were staring fascinated at the stage as Ken started to speak.

'I'd like to propose Robin Hawkes. He's the only one of us who's got off his bum and done some research, and he can talk the nuclear language from the inside. I'd be much better employed making a noise on the sidelines. Stuntman, that's me!'

So Robin Hawkes became chairman, and Pam Webb's husband Jim agreed to be treasurer. People were asked to give a contribution of a pound that evening if they could.

'I haven't got any cash on me,' said Guy as he fumbled in his pockets.

'We're broke anyway.' Nick sat back on the table, which promptly collapsed causing a minor diversion.

Hawkes stood up, taking no notice of the noise. 'I'd like to explain why a physicist like myself is standing here.'

'Here we go,' muttered Alan.

'Firstly, I'm here because I'm wary of the way the nuclear industry interprets its data. Everything in the nuclear garden is a lot too rosy. A scientist is always supposed to be pessimistic, over-careful; his job is to assess all the worst possible effects before he comes up with any solutions. What happens in the nuclear industry is the opposite. The assumptions are always optimistic, the data are always interpreted in the most liberal and unscientific way. For example, we are assured that low-level waste is not harmful to health and will anyway be contained so that it can't escape. Fine. But I know that little exhaustive research has been done on radioactive effects, and *no* analysis has yet been done on a trench burial that's supposed to contain its dangerous contents for *three hundred years*. How can safety be claimed so confidently for such a new unproven technology?'

People murmured assent, craning their necks in total attention. Someone shouted: 'But surely they wouldn't do it if it wasn't safe?' Hawkes ignored him.

'And what do we all feel when the head of our nuclear industry says a Chernobyl-type accident couldn't happen here? We know it's an unscientific statement, based on the most favourable reading of data. Would you buy a used car from a man like that? Come to think of it, would you even buy a new one?'

There was laughter, loudest from Ken, who banged the table and said 'Very good' audibly to Pam Webb. The boys groaned.

'Second, I'm here because so very little is really known about radiation. We should be giving it research priority. Instead, we behave like ostriches and use words like "incredible" and "unbelievable" and "impossible" when the spectre of a nuclear

38

accident here is touched on; if it happens, we are totally unprepared.'

There was a break for a few minutes while people asked Hawkes questions. Then the American, Mark Ableman, stood up.

'I used to live near Three Mile Island, and I entirely agree with Robin here about the way the nuclear industry will not face up to reality. I'll tell you a true story. Some people my family knew well ran a farm for breeding exotic birds; the farm was situated not far from TMI. Now, just after the nuclear accident there in seventy-nine over four hundred birds died in one single day. Our friends had never had a disaster like this before. There was nothing to explain it, except the one thing. Radiation. They started a case against TMI. And their case was dismissed because it was held, against the evidence, that those birds died from being asphyxiated by something in the ventilation system. No one would accept it was radiation. It was unbelievable. I could tell you a dozen more stories.' From the looks on many faces, he would have to, in a lengthy session in the George and Dragon.

'There's just one final thing I have to say. Don't accept the statistics. Robin's right. They just monkey about with the data until it sounds good. We were told that there was no meltdown of the TMI radio-active core. We were told that the temperature in the reactor never reached 2,500 degrees, the point when the area should have been evacuated. Five years later — five years too late — we learnt that TMI had a partial meltdown and was only half an hour from total meltdown. Temperature in the core? It reached 5,100 degrees. You don't ever forget lies like that.'

The silent hall gazed at the plump American, many of them wondering how much radiation sat in his cheerful well-fed body, waiting to erupt.

Guy leant across and whispered: 'I've got to go. Come and play tennis, Alan. I'll get in touch.'

Alan and Nick had by now had enough of the meeting, and they followed Guy out and saw him drive away with a spurt of loose chippings.

'Lucky bastard. I wouldn't mind a nice new Golf. What are we going to do with the rest of the evening?' asked Nick.

'Take off in the general direction of Maldham. Shall we use your car or mine?'

'I think we'd better take both, don't you? We can have a riotous time racing each other, my deah.'

They got on their bikes and headed out of Stagwell, their lights glowing feebly in the darkness, their voices carrying clearly in the still night air.

Maddy, strolling around with Sally Dews, heard them pass and kept out of sight. 'They've been to that meeting,' she said, touching her shorn head. She had had it cut short as a boy's with a longer tuft in front. Her hair was thick enough to stand on end without help; she kept running her hand over the top. 'It feels like a soft brush.'

'You are lucky to have such thick hair. It looks really good. If I had that cut, I'd look bald.'

They continued to discuss hairstyles as they wandered towards the centre of Stagwell. As they neared the church, people started pouring out of the adjacent hall, many of them aiming for the pub. Maddy and Sally sat on a wall and watched the crowd disperse.

'Hundreds of people seem to have gone,' said Maddy. 'There's Mr Hawkes with Ken Pope. And the vicar. All the anti-nuke nutters.'

'Dad thinks everyone is making a stupid fuss about this dump.' Sally's father was an engineer at the power station. 'He says it won't make any difference to Stagwell's safety. It's only low-level waste, and it's got to be stored somewhere. Why not here?'

'Alan's got his knickers in a twist about the whole nuclear bit. He was even telling me it was dangerous to go out today because of the Chernobyl fallout.'

'You must be joking. Tell him he probably gets a bigger dose of radiation from his luminous watch.' Sally snorted and got off the wall. 'Dad's afraid that this issue is going to divide Stagwell. Considering we've lived all these years happily with the power station right beside us, he's a bit fed up that people have suddenly got so excited.'

A moped went slowly past them and stopped in front of St George's Hall, which was now locked up. The rider hesitated and then turned and came back to the girls.

'Do you happen to know where the meeting about the nuclear-waste dump is?' asked a female voice. Otherwise the rider was well disguised behind helmet and clothing.

'It was there and it's over. They've just finished.'

'Blast.'

'The organisers are all in the pub.' Maddy jerked her head in the direction of the George and Dragon.

The rider took no notice of this remark, but stared moodily into the distance. She had a very white face and green eyes.

'What did the meeting decide to do?' she said suddenly.

'No idea,' replied Maddy. 'We didn't go.'

There was no mistaking the scorn in the girl's eyes as she thanked them for their help and drove off. Maddy turned to Sally.

'You know who that was, don't you?'

'Couldn't see behind the helmet.'

'Kathy Wilson, Janice's sister.'

'What's she doing, wandering round Stagwell looking for the meeting? They don't even live in Stagwell.'

'Janice says she's crazy.'

'Let's go back to my place. I'm tired of hanging about in case Jonathan appears. He can go to hell for all I care.'

FOUR
Sunday, 4 May

Angie came over at one o'clock from the Norringtons'
for her children. Alan and Maddy were still in bed,
so she shouted at them to get up and get dressed at
once. She took an unwilling Luke with her over the
road.

'What are we having for lunch?' muttered Luke.
'I hope it's good.'

'I've no idea, but it smells like roast beef. Delicious
anyway.'

'They prob'ly like it all bloody. It makes me feel
sick when it's bloody.'

'Luke, stop suffering before you have to.'

Alan and Maddy followed ten minutes later,
equally unwillingly. They were led into a room with
pale green walls and carpet and so many plants that
even the light seemed green.

'Now, Alan and Maddy, a soft drink or some
white wine?' asked Paul, flashing his professional

43

smile. They both chose wine, Maddy rather aggressively with an eye on her mother. The glasses were so fine they threatened to snap in their hands. Alan and Maddy sat down together on a spotless white sofa. Everything in the room was perfect; perfectly placed, perfectly clean. Their grubby old trainers looked wrong on the new dust-free carpet. Alan spilled a drop of wine on the white sofa, and moved his legs so that his jeans mopped it up while hiding it.

'Well, this is very nice,' said Paul heartily. 'I think it's the first time we've entertained teenagers in this house, isn't it, darling? Tell us about yourselves. Angie says you've got exams very soon.'

'Yes,' said Alan.

'Too soon.'

They had a creaking conversation about subjects. Alan drained his glass, which Paul promptly refilled, saying 'You don't mind?' to Angie as he did so.

'Mind what?'

'Him having another glass.'

'Fine by me.'

Alan did not like the way Paul referred to him as 'him' and began to feel Paul was a condescending creep. He swung his glass up and saw to his horror he'd spilt more wine on the wretched white sofa. He moved again to cover it up. The three adults were in the middle of a familiar conversation about the absence of alcohol in their teenage lives. The three Page offspring sat in silence waiting for food. Luke finished every crumb of a bowl of small cheese biscuits, and then stared fixedly at his hostess. Either because she noticed or because the food was ready anyway, Elaine Norrington got up at this point and within minutes called them to the dining-room.

Elaine served very good food: lots of roast beef (well done) and a heap of individual crisp Yorkshire puddings. Luke had four, and there were still plenty left over. There was a mountain of browned roast potatoes, and masses of gravy to pour over three sorts of vegetable.

'I thought trad food would go down best,' said Elaine, watching Luke with evident pleasure. He never even looked up.

After Paul carved second helpings, Alan suddenly asked: 'What do you feel about the proposed nuclear-waste dump, Mr Norrington?' His mother was frowning at him, but he took no notice.

'The hot topic in Stagwell.' Paul smiled. 'And there was a protest meeting last night, I hear.'

'I went, actually. But you haven't said what your views are.'

'Well, I feel people are over-reacting, to be honest. It's only a test drilling, after all. Nothing is finalised. And the people of Stagwell have lived happily all these years in the lee of a nuclear power station—'

'Not happily. Not any more—'

'Don't exaggerate, Alan.' Angie was still frowning at him. 'Most people are perfectly happy about it.'

'Were. They aren't any more. You should have heard them last night.'

'But the safety record at Stagwell is excellent,' said Paul. 'There has never been a major incident.'

'There's always a first time. And you could be lying to us. There could have been lots of leaks and we'd never know. Luckily for you, radioactivity is invisible.'

Paul smiled his let's-humour-this-nutter smile. 'But why should we lie to you? What evidence is there that we have?'

'I'm not an expert, Mr Norrington.'

'Paul. Please call me Paul.'

'But we all know that the nuclear industry is

famous for presenting statistics so that they look really good. You never take the worst-case scenario, always the best.'

'I know everyone's very sensitive at the moment because of Chernobyl—'

'And what about the *Observer* today?' said Elaine, with a curious air of triumph. Paul frowned at her, but she went on: 'I'll just get it.'

'Why not wait—?' Paul made a despairing face at Angie as Elaine disappeared through the door. 'Trust Elaine to start up a red herring.'

Elaine came back into the room and started to read out loud.

'*An explosion at Dungeness Power Station in Kent has been kept secret for over a month by officials of the Central Electricity Board.*

'*The disclosure comes in a week when ministers — including the Prime Minister — have emphasised Britain's openness in nuclear matters. . . .*'

Elaine sounded gleeful. 'Oh dear, heads will roll.'

'It was only a small leak, nothing dangerous. It happened in a bypass system, not in the main reactor.' He looked very cool, but Alan was sure he wanted to leap at his wife and rip the newspaper out of her hands. Even Maddy, who had been staring out of the window, was paying attention.

'How much radioactivity was released?' she asked. Before Paul could answer, Elaine read out: '*About 110 lb of mildly radioactive gas was released*. Mildly radioactive sounds nice, doesn't it — as if the air would feel full of zing as a result?' Taking no notice of her husband's furious expression, she handed the paper to Alan and started clearing plates.

'Listen to this,' said Alan. '*Only by immense good fortune was a large release of reactor gas avoided. How did a piece of nuclear equipment that had been*

46

subject to all the CEGBs current design analysis end up failing so spectacularly?'

'Good question,' said Paul. 'Good question, very good question. And there has been an exhaustive inquiry into it, believe me. It's not the sort of failure we want to happen again.'

'But it will; it's bound to.'

'It's very unlikely. We learn from our mistakes.' Paul smiled his fixed smile.

'But—'

'Alan, please. Paul knows these things from the inside, you're just picking up comments from a newspaper—'

'It doesn't mean the newspaper isn't right.'

'There's bound to be a lot of exaggeration at the moment, Alan,' said Paul placatingly. 'People have been frightened by Chernobyl, and rightly so—'

'Haven't you?'

'Haven't I what?'

'Felt fear because of Chernobyl? Don't you sometimes think as you drive down that road to the power station that it could happen here?'

'The Magnox reactor is in no way comparable to the light-water reactor at Chernobyl—'

'You're not answering my question.'

'Alan, please,' Angie interrupted.

'Let the boy talk,' said Paul.

Alan gritted his teeth. He could see that Paul was losing his cool, too.

'My question is this: don't you admit that tomorrow it could happen here, that one day it *will* happen somewhere in England, and we'll all be irradiated to blazes? Doesn't that make you lose sleep?'

'Look, Alan, I damned well know the risks, and they don't bother me. I know that every reactor has a theoretical risk of one major accident per ten thousand years of operating life. No reactor operates for ten thousand years, so the theoretical risk to each reactor is even more remote. It's an acceptable risk. I risk far more just getting into my car and driving on the roads.' Paul smiled at Angie, who gave a nervous little smile back while trying to frown at Alan. Maddy kicked Alan on the leg; he glared at her and took no notice.

'I can see why you're not frightened of the *theoretical* risk. It all sounds so unlikely: once in a thousand years—'

'Even better, ten thousand years.'

'But that's just theory; in practice, it could happen *any time* in the ten thousand years — next year, tomorrow. That's the real risk, isn't it?'

'Well, in a way—'

'What I'd like to know is how the figure of ten thousand years is worked out. Using what data?'

Paul stared at him, obviously at a loss. 'I'm not sure how it was originally calculated, but I'm sure it would have been based on carefully assessed figures. What on earth has happened to Elaine and the dessert?'

'My physics teacher was at the meeting last night. He said the reason he was supporting an anti-dumping protest was because . . . er, because you interpret data too liberally — that this was unscientific. Your calculations were therefore unreliable, he said.'

'I must just see if Elaine—'

'But do you agree?'

'I see his point, but I don't agree with him. Look, Alan, this conversation is getting us nowhere. You're obviously heavily biased by what I call the Greenpeace Syndrome, and I'm employed by the nuclear industry. We're unlikely to agree, but I think you ought to find out more about the nuclear industry before you condemn it outright. Come and look round Stagwell power station. Then you can see for yourself how efficient, clean and safe it is.'

'I'll come, too,' said Angie. 'I'd be fascinated. I'm sure Maddy and Luke would be, too.'

'Fine. We'll arrange a family visit. Where *is* our dessert?'

'Don't forget, Mr Norrington,' said Alan, 'that on Friday, the twenty-fifth of April, Chernobyl looked efficient, clean and safe. I'm sure people were saying just that as they were being shown round the reactor.'

The door swung open, and Elaine entered, triumphantly bearing a large flat dish. On it was a white hump, browned at the edges, looking like a large light-coloured slug.

'Baked Alaska!' she exclaimed. 'My own ice-cream inside. Quick, everyone, before it starts to melt.'

'I'm really angry with you, Alan. You were awful, arguing like that with Paul when you were his guest. It was very rude. You went on and on, obsessed with your own point of view.' Angie paced up and down the front room. 'And when he offered to show you round the reactor you didn't even bother to answer or say thank you.'

'I don't particularly want to go.'

'There's still no need to be rude. You were very aggressive.'

'He's a creep.'

'Alan, he is not.' Angie's face grew pink, and her eyes flashed. 'He's an extremely nice man, and you're a boorish teenager.'

'It's my age, Mother dear. How can I help it? I told you not to take us. All teenagers are boorish, untidy, thoughtless, selfish, noisy, and have smelly socks.'

'The Baked Alaska was yummy,' said Luke

dreamily. 'That was ace, that meal. Do you think they'll ask us again?'

'Not a chance,' said Alan.

'Why not?'

Angie suddenly hugged Luke. 'Oh, Luke, Luke, you're so sweet.' She pressed her cheek against Luke's hair. He disengaged himself gently but firmly.

'Do you think we could make Baked Alaska?'

'I don't see why not. I'm sure Elaine would give you the recipe if you asked her nicely.'

'OK.' And, before she realised what he was doing, Luke had run across the road and rung the Norringtons' bell. Five minutes later he returned waving a sheet of paper.

'She typed it out for me straight away. She said the secret was to have the oven very hot.' He smiled to himself. 'Hot as a nuclear reactor.'

THE KETTLE THAT BECAME A KILLER

Chernobyl is now a ghost city. The deadly cloud has taken away the homes of 50,000 people.

And the fire is still smouldering. Soviet troops are risking their lives in dramatic fire-fighting. They are dropping sand, lead and boron from helicopters in a desperate attempt to control the radioactive furnace. . . .

Daily News

FIVE
Monday, 5 May

'Dad punched Ron Dews on the nose last night.' Nick was sitting beside Alan on the bus, trying to finish his French homework. 'Is *mer le* or *la*?'

'*La*. What caused the fight?'

'Ron came round to collect some manure, and said rude things about the anti-dump protests. Things like the dump would be no more radioactive than the load of shit he'd just put in the car. Dad said the shit was probably more radioactive than he realised, and the discussion grew heated. Ma and I lurked in the kitchen, waiting for the shouting to end. The next thing we hear is a yell, and there's Ron sitting in the manure heap with a bruised nose. We had our work cut out to calm him down. And clean him down. Ma was mad with Dad. She says if he's so belligerent towards people who think differently about the dump he'll turn Stagwell into a battleground. "And I tell

51

you, Ken Pope, if that happens, I'd rather have nuclear contamination and be done with it." ' Nick imitated his mother's Scots accent to perfection.

'I had a bit of a row yesterday on the same subject.' Alan told Nick about his talk with Paul Norrington. 'I got him hopping.'

'But you didn't land him one, like Dad. Just as well. All this aggro will give us a bad name. This can't be right. "*J'ai pris mes choses pour nager, et je vais à la mer pour baigner.*" '

'*Baigner* is reflexive. *Pour se baigner*. And you've got your tenses all muddled up.'

'God, how I hate French. So what do I put — "*j'ai allé a la mer*"?'

' "*Je suis allé. . . .*" '

'I'm going to get a great mark for this load of cobblers. What is more, I'm going to fail the exam,' Nick groaned as he corrected his work.

As they got off the bus, they passed a newspaper-stand near the school gates. Headlines screamed: *British Milk and Water Contaminated*. They turned into the playground and found a large handwritten notice on the drinking-fountain which read DANGER: DO NOT DRINK.

'This is over the top,' announced Alan. He lifted the notice and drank several mouthfuls. He started splashing water at Nick, who retaliated. Then Alan suddenly clutched his chest and began to die in agony. He was famous for his slow-motion death scenes; a crowd collected round him. Amongst them he noticed Kathy Wilson, who stood swinging her crash helmet and watching with a half-smile.

'What's killing you this time, Alan?' asked a new arrival.

'Acute radiation sickness,' Alan managed to gasp out before collapsing into a twitching heap. Out of the corner of his eye he saw Kathy walk away as he completed his death throes. A teacher moved everyone on, and with an annoyed expression replaced the notice on the fountain.

'By the way,' said Nick, as he and Alan parted for different lessons, 'there's a meeting on Thursday evening, and Dad says he'd like us to be there. It's for planning some action. He says it will be good.'

'Thursday's my worst day for homework.'

'Try to come.'

'I'll have to play it by ear.'

'Becquerels, roentgens, sieverts, rems. I'm in such a muddle. Why can't they get their act together and have just one way of measuring radioactivity?' moaned Janice.

'I sometimes feel that every country uses a different measurement on purpose to confuse us,' said Mr Hawkes. 'But I'll try to clarify it for you. The old unit of dose of radiation was called the Roentgen after the German physicist who discovered X-rays. Since this measurement was made in air and not in people, it was changed to REM which simply means Roentgen Equivalent Man. So a millirem, for instance, is a thousandth of a rem. The becquerel, also called after a physicist, measures the rate of spontaneous radioactive decay — one becquerel equals one disintegration per second. Finally, the sievert is a new international word and it's equal to a hundred rems.'

'Would a hundred rems kill you?' asked Alan.

'Not immediately, but you'd be likely to develop a fatal cancer in time.'

'What's the killer dose?'

'A thousand rems and over.'

'Sir, I saw a headline this morning and it said something about the danger of a Chinese syndrome.

53

What are they on about?' This came from Christopher Stillwell, who usually paid no attention whatever to lessons. He looked annoyed when some people laughed and shouted: 'China Syndrome — it's a film — with Jane Fonda.'

'OK, tell Christopher what the name means. You were shouting loudest, Ginger. You tell him.'

'Never saw the film, sir.'

'Someone else. Kevin.'

'It's about a full meltdown, when the whole core is on fire in this power station and it burns through the floor and goes down into the water-table and contaminates a huge chunk of America.'

'That frightening prospect is looming at Chernobyl. As far as we can gather the core is still burning. They're pouring heavy weights of sand, lead and boron on to it in an attempt to put the fire out. They have no choice, although they know that under all this weight the concrete base could give way. Then the ultimate nightmare starts — rivers and streams take the contamination far further than the original area of the catastrophe and there's no controlling the disaster for years to come.'

'Mr Hawkes, isn't there a reservoir under Chernobyl?' asked Alan.

'Yes, there is. Nobody has got round to explaining why there is; all we know is that they're desperately trying to drain it in case the worst happens. Does anybody have an idea how long the reactor core will stay radioactive?'

The class looked at their notes. Maddy answered.

'Caesium 137 has a half-life of thirty years, so does Strontium 90. Carbon 14 has a half-life of 5,730 years, and plutonium remains deadly for 250,000 years.'

There was a silence.

'It's horrible.'

'A China Syndrome may never happen.' This came from Sally Dews.

'Let's hope for the sake of us all it doesn't. I personally feel that, given that there are now about three hundred and seventy reactors round the world, it's very likely that somewhere, some time, it will.'

There was another silence.

'Any questions?'

'Sir, the power station at Stagwell. It's much safer than Chernobyl, isn't it?' The questioner was Elspeth Riley, a small pale girl who hardly ever spoke. Robin Hawkes hesitated. The rustle of chatter died down as the class waited for his reply.

'In actual fact, Elspeth, it isn't.'

'My dad says it is,' said Sally.

Instead of replying, Hawkes turned to the blackboard and drew three boxlike shapes, and pointed to the first. 'First, the Russian RMBK reactor. This has three levels of containment, of protection: a steel pressure vessel round the reactor core and two reinforced concrete shells. Second, the Magnox reactor, like ours at Stagwell. The reactor itself has primary steel and secondary concrete containment, but the latter is only partial. In other words, the gas coolant circuit is not fully protected, and this is a fundamental weakness in all Magnox reactors. The noise you hear all the time in Stagwell is caused by the circulating gas coolant, by the way. Third, the Advanced Gas-cooled Reactor or AGR. The AGRs have one single massive reinforced concrete containment. There's no secondary shell, because the accepted view is that a breach in such a massive wall is too incredible to imagine.' Hawkes turned round and raised his hands. 'But now the incredible has happened.'

'Shouldn't our station be closed down, then, since

it's old?' asked Elspeth. The class had never heard her say so much.

'Yes, by rights it should. But don't forget it's there to make money, so they won't close it down until they're forced.'

'My dad says it's got years of life yet.' Sally's face was red. 'So if it can go on making money why shouldn't it? You don't work there, sir, you don't know what good condition it's in.'

'A lot of people would lose their jobs and all if they closed it down.'

'We could all lose a lot more than our jobs if they don't—'

'But they'll close it down before it becomes dangerous; they wouldn't take stupid risks—'

'They didn't manage to close down Chernobyl.'

Everyone was joining in the argument; for once, no one heard the lesson-bell. Hawkes had to wave for quiet. As soon as he'd achieved it, Elspeth Riley said: 'I live in Stagwell, and I'm scared of that power station, I really am.'

'Give over, Elspeth,' shouted Sally. 'Don't exaggerate. The station's dead safe—'

'*Dead* safe—'

'You can say that again—'

Mr Hawkes had to push his pupils out of the laboratory in the end, telling Elspeth as she passed to ask Alan or Nick about the new protest group.

As the class packed up and left the room, Elspeth made for Nick. He and Alan had long ago christened her the Weasel; her sly beady eyes and pinched face looked just like a weasel's.

'Tell us about this group, then.'

'You should have come to the meeting last Saturday.'

'I didn't hear nothing about it. When's the next meeting?'

'Don't know. Keep a look out for posters.' Nick was offhand.

'You will tell me as well, won't you? I don't want to miss it.' She fixed him with her earnest beady gaze.

'OK.' Nick edged away.

'Promise?'

'Yeah, I promise.'

As Elspeth went off, Nick muttered: 'Anything to get rid of her. I hope she loses interest. I don't think I could stand being too near Elspeth Riley.'

'Hell, I'm knackered,' said Alan. 'Lessons all morning. Let's go and get a coffee.'

There was a scrum round the dispensers. The largest queue was for coffee, so Alan and Nick opted for soup. A pinkish-yellow fluid filled their plastic beakers. Alan sniffed his, and tasted it gingerly. 'This stuff bears as much resemblance to soup as I do to Mick Jagger. Ah, well, down the hatch. Hope we don't puke.'

'What have you got next? I've got a free.'

'Art. Quick, beat it; the Weasel is making tracks in this direction, and her eye is definitely fixed on you.'

Alan and Maddy were listening to music in Alan's room that evening. Angie had gone to the cinema with the Norringtons; Luke was in bed.

'We haven't heard from Dad for a while,' said Maddy suddenly. She was lying back on the carpet with her eyes shut. 'Not since before Easter.'

'The gaps get longer and longer.'

'I'd like to go and see him.'

'He hasn't exactly pressed us to go out there.'

'I don't want him to become a stranger; I couldn't bear it.'

Alan almost said he was one already, but thought better of it.

'Alan, do you think Mum will ever get married again?'

'Haven't a clue.'

'She hasn't had a single boyfriend since Dad left.'

'As far as we know.'

'We'd know. Mum's not good at hiding things. I can see, for instance, that she likes Paul Norrington more than she should, considering he's married.'

'I can't understand what she sees in him.'

'He's all right.' Maddy tapped her feet against the wall in time to the rhythm. 'But it's a horrible thought, her getting married again. Imagine if she married someone with kids, teenaged kids like us. We'd have to start thinking about them as our brothers and sisters. Ugh. I'd hate it. I think I'd leave home.'

'So would I.'

'Then she'd have another baby.'

'She'd be too old, wouldn't she?'

'No, she wouldn't. She's only thirty-nine, and lots of women have babies older than that.'

'I can't bear even thinking about it.'

'It happens all the time.'

'Shut up, Maddy. Leave the subject alone. I've had enough.'

'Now you know how I feel when you go on and on about nuclear danger.'

'But that's real, and it affects us all. At least what happens to Mum only affects you, Luke and me.'

The estuary looked strangely flat and wide. Hundreds of boats were out, and though none of them had sails they whizzed around like wasps on a jammy table. The power station was tilting, slowly tilting towards the sea; the earth, no longer solid, was bubbling at its sides. People were climbing in thousands out of the top of the reactors, screaming. As the reactors sank and disappeared, the bubbling earth covered the screaming people. Yet the estuary remained flat, and the boats circled about, taking no notice of the catastrophe nearby. Slowly the earth started to bubble and gape in wider areas: Stagwell Quay started sinking, Stagwell itself loosened and gaped. . . . The smell was terrible, a scorched bitter stink with an undertone of sulphur. The smell attacked the human skin, making it flake and burn. . . .

Maddy woke in a state of horror, sweating and terrified. The smell still seemed to linger in her nostrils; her skin crawled. She leapt out of bed, trying to shake herself free of her nightmare. That smell, that smell. . . . She put her head out of the window. She could still see those strange boats circling as if maddened on the sea. . . .

The whine of the power station bit into her consciousness. The fresh air did not calm her. She decided to go downstairs and make herself a drink. If Alan's light was on, she'd go and talk to him — then she saw it was after two o'clock. Well, she'd make the drink. She went downstairs, and found the hall light still on. She was surprised; Angie was very careful with electricity — she couldn't afford not to be.

Maddy decided that the best drink to banish that smell would be a cup of hot Marmite. She was boiling the kettle and licking Marmite off a spoon as she waited, enjoying the strong salty taste, when the front door opened. Angie came in, and jumped in surprise when she saw her daughter.

'You gave me such a shock. I thought you'd all be asleep.' Angie was pale.

'I woke up. You're back late.'

'I know. I shall be useless at work tomorrow. Oh, well.'

'Did you enjoy the film?'

'Yes, we did, thanks. At least, Paul and I did. Elaine had a headache and stayed at home.' Angie yawned hugely. 'Good night, love. Switch off all the lights, won't you?'

'Yes, of course. 'Night.'

Angie suddenly gave her daughter a fervent hug; as they did not touch each other much, this was unexpected. Maddy, still on edge from her nightmare, was stiff. She held her Marmitey spoon carefully at arm's length.

'You are a funny old thing,' said Angie. 'Sleep well.'

'Goodnight, Mum.' Maddy poured water into her mug and sipped her drink with pleasure. She sat at the kitchen table, unwilling to go upstairs quite yet. The memory of the smell still lingered. At last, when the drink was finished, she put off the lights and climbed the dark stairs. As she passed her mother's room, she thought she heard her crying.

TWILIGHT OF THE NUCLEAR GOD
Most people recognise intuitively what seems impossible for many engineers to admit: all machines have the capacity to fail, and complex machines do so in ways their designers do not anticipate.

The impact of a nuclear accident is so huge that the world cannot afford not to learn from its own mistakes. A Chernobyl here might have devastated half of England and Wales; a Chernobyl in France, with the wind in the right direction, might also have devastated half of England and Wales. . . .

The Observer

SIX
Thursday, 8 May

The meeting on Thursday evening was at the Popes' farm. Alan did as much work as he could but still had an hour's worth to do when he left the house. Angie heard him get his bike out.

'Where are you off to?'

'Just down to Nick's.'

'Have you finished your homework?'

'Sort of.'

'Why do you have to go there anyway? You'll be seeing Nick tomorrow.'

'Er, I need to get a book off him.'

'Alan, I wish you'd get yourself better organised — and, anyway, can't Maddy help—?'

'She doesn't do geography.'

Alan managed to escape at last. He hadn't told his mother about the meeting because he was sure she'd have stopped him. He took the flat boring road, and was passed by Robin Hawkes who tooted and waved a hand. When he arrived he found Hawkes, Mark Ableman, the Webbs and Ken Pope sitting in the stiff and rarely used parlour. Nick was in a corner, and Alan joined him. There was a heated discussion going on between Ken and Pam.

'I don't know the rights and wrongs of what happened, but what I *do* know is that Ron Dews is going round saying we're a bunch of lunatic extremists—'

'He'll change his tune when we get our campaign going,' blustered Ken.

'You shouldn't have hit him.'

'Did you actually exchange blows?' Mark Ableman looked worried.

'It was only a gentle tap. . . .'

'Not so gentle if the poor man landed in the manure heap,' muttered Nick.

'Oh dear,' said Mark Ableman. But everyone in the room smiled guiltily.

'No more gentle taps, I promise. Even if Ron Dews hits me first.'

Robin got the meeting started, and it was quickly decided that a petition should be organised to see how much local support their campaign actually had.

'Could you get it going, Pam? Make sure it's widely circulated. It won't cut any ice unless it's a massive representation.' Robin looked excited. 'We must publicise it properly — take space in the local papers if necessary. Then we must deliver it ourselves to Downing Street, with maximum publicity. Publicity — who's going to handle publicity?'

'I'll do that if you like,' said Mark. 'I've run pressure groups in the States; I know the sort of approach that's needed, and the importance of timing. We need national as well as local coverage. Particularly television.'

'And we need hard cash.' Jim Webb looked gloomy. 'We collected forty-eight quid at the door the other night. I've opened an account, by the way; for want of anything better, I've called it the No-to-Nirex account.' Everyone laughed, but Jim stayed gloomy. Alan wondered if he ever smiled. 'But forty-eight quid isn't going to get us very far. I think we need a fund-raising event.'

While the group discussed boring things like jumble sales, Nick and Alan went to the kitchen to make tea and coffee.

'Do you really think television reporters are going to bother to come down to sleepy old Stagwell-in-the-sticks to do a programme on us?'

'No idea.' Alan sat on the kitchen table, while Nick stacked a motley selection of mugs on a tray. The kettle was hissing slightly on the Aga hot-plate, a long way off boiling. The front of the battered old Aga was festooned with an amazing number of socks; Haggis the cat was busy playing with these until they slipped off the rail on to the floor.

'I suppose it partly depends on us. Dad wants the two of us to think up as many good ideas as possible, ideas that'll really catch the eye. He's had a brilliant one.'

'What?' The cat finally brought down the last sock, and curled itself up on the heap.

'Sir Oliver Winter's got a hot-air balloon, right? Dad wants him to trail a long banner from it saying NO DUMPING. Just imagine how many people would see that.'

'Great.'

'The action's got to hot up the moment we know the date they start test drilling.'

'What about getting people to put NO TO NIREX on their sails? Not just the fishing boats; summer's nearly here, and everyone with a boat will be on the water at weekends.'

'Not bad, Alan.'

At that moment Nick's mother Jean came in.

'Oh, hullo, Alan, I didn't know you were in on all this.'

'I sort of got dragged in—'

'Look at that cat, will you? He drives me mad. Haggis, if you do that again I'll murder you.' She threw the cat out of the back door and hung up the socks again. 'The kettle's boiling. I take it you boys are so well up in your revision that you can spare the time to help hatch plots to bring the entire nuclear industry to its knees?'

They hurried off with the tray and kettle, Alan whispering to Nick before they entered the parlour: 'Isn't your mum in favour, then?'

'She's like Maddy. Sitting on the fence.'

By the weekend, Nick and Alan found they had been press-ganged by Pam Webb into going round a housing estate at the edge of Stagwell to collect names for the petition. Both were horrified at the thought of having to knock on doors and ask people's opinions. They offered to do their school instead, but Pam would not listen.

'Robin is organising the Maldham area. I need you to help in Stagwell.'

Alan looked pleadingly at Pam's round cheer- ful face. 'Pam, I've never done this kind of thing before. People are bound to say no just because we're teenagers—'

'Stuff and nonsense,' said Pam. 'You and Nick are going to be successful. Everyone will be impressed that young people like you care enough to get involved. They'll sign, you'll see.'

'If they open the door in the first place,' groaned Nick. 'They'll look through their net curtains and think we've come to mug them.'

Pam laughed. 'Stop moaning, the pair of you. Come on, it's a challenge. Have a bash today, and if it really goes badly wrong come and see me this evening and I'll try to find someone else. Mind you, we're very short of helpers. . . .'

Pam drove off in her orange Cortina with WEBBS MINICAB SERVICE on one side and SAFE SPEED IS YOUR NEED on the other. She left the boys with a clipboard each on which were sheets of paper headed: *SCAND: Stagwell Campaign Against Nuclear Dumping.*

'I didn't realise they'd come up with a name,' said Alan. 'SCAND. Not bad.'

'Let's fake a whole lot of names,' said Nick. 'Nobody at Downing Street would know the difference.'

'Pam Webb would. Besides, it's quite difficult to invent a variety of signatures—'

'I wasn't serious. I just don't want to bloody do this. I don't mind the stunts — they could be fun — but, hell, going round Sunningdale housing estate. . . . I can't think of a worse way of spending a Saturday morning.'

They set off on foot, gloomily discussing what they would say at each door. Sunningdale had been built in the last five years and was an estate of semi-detached bungalows, some of them looking very tidy and smart and others already paintworn and seedy. The boys decided to keep together to start with; Nick pushed Alan into ringing a doorbell first. A man with a heavy stubble and a collarless old shirt came to the door and opened it a few centimetres.

'Yes?'

'We're representing SCAND, the campaign against nuclear dumping in Stagwell, and we wondered what your views were on the subject,' gabbled Alan.

'Bloody cheek.' Alan was ready to retreat as the man opened the door further, when he realised the man was not referring to him. 'We've already got a power station. What we don't need is any more nuclear what's-its. They never ask us, do they?'

'Here's your chance to make your voice heard. Sign the SCAND petition. It's going to be delivered to Downing Street when we've got enough names.' Alan held out his board.

'Why not? Give us the pen.' He wrote with care a spider's web of a signature, and then said: 'Good luck. There's some on this estate that won't sign, but most will. Avoid number fifteen — they both work at Stagwell Mound.'

Encouraged by this start, Nick went to the other side of the street, and the two boys worked slowly along the houses. Sometimes it was a simple yes or no; at others, lengthy discussions and arguments took place. Once or twice a curtain twitched but no one answered. After an hour they met in the middle of a road to compare notes.

'Six people signed in the last house,' said Nick triumphantly. 'I've used up over a sheet; that's thirty-seven signatures.'

'Fantastic. I've only got twenty-nine.'

A man walked past them; Alan leapt towards him, causing him to pull up, startled and apprehensive.

'Sorry about that; I didn't mean to give you a shock. I just thought you might be interested in signing this petition against the nuclear dump. . . .'

The man was still suspicious. 'Who are you?' By

the time Alan had finished explaining and the man had signed without much enthusiasm, Nick had done two more houses. Alan then went to a corner house, very neat and tidy; its name, *Eastbourne*, was carved on an oval piece of wood stuck into the bright green, closely cut lawn. There was a collection of shiny painted gnomes clustered round a red and white concrete toadstool. Alan almost gave the house a miss, but told himself gnomes didn't necessarily mean you'd be pro-nuclear. He rang the bell, which played the tune of 'The Blue Bells of Scotland'. In the middle of this, the door opened and the Weasel stared out at him.

'Er, hullo, Elspeth.' Alan cursed his bad luck as he backed away slightly. Elspeth smiled at him eagerly.

'Have you come to tell me about a meeting?' Her beady eyes shone. She was wearing a bright pink tracksuit with Mickey Mouse on the front.

'No, I've come with this petition which I know you'll sign.' He pushed the board and biro at her, hoping she'd sign quickly so that he could escape. Out of the corner of his eye he saw Nick duck out of sight.

'Oh, this is wonderful,' breathed the Weasel. 'Of course I'll sign. SCAND. What a good name. I'll get Mum and Dad to sign, too, and my little brother. Come in a minute.'

'No, I'll just wait here, thanks all the same.' Alan looked for Nick, but he remained invisible. A couple of the gnomes stared at Alan. Then the Weasel reappeared, waving the petition.

'Gran signed, too. That's five names.'

'Great. Thanks. Now, I must push on—'

'Look, can't I help collect signatures? I'd really like to help the cause—'

'I'll have to ask the organiser—'

'You tell me who it is and I'll ask them myself.'

Elspeth was the sort of girl who had learnt from bitter experience not to rely on other people.

Alan swallowed. He knew she was needed. 'Go and see Pam Webb. She has the minicab service.'

' "Safe speed is your need," ' recited Elspeth. 'We've got her number. . . .'

Alan caught a brief glimpse of Nick, lurking in a driveway. 'You ring her, then, and she'll tell you what to do.'

'Brilliant. This is really brilliant—'

'Look, I've got to go.'

Elspeth followed him down the path. Her pink tracksuit clashed horribly with the red gnomes. She watched him go along the pavement, making it impossible for him to join Nick. So he canvassed another house and found to his relief she'd gone inside when he returned to the street. He found Nick in a driveway, still laughing. Alan gave him a push.

'Shut up.'

'It's the funniest thing I've seen in years. Alan disturbing the Weasel in her lair.'

'Weasels don't have lairs; they have sets—'

'Badgers have sets. Weasels have. . . .' Nick started laughing again. 'Weasels have houses called Eastbourne with gnomes. . . .' He doubled up, cackling so much he couldn't go on.

A shout came from behind them. 'Get off that drive; that's private property. Just because I signed your petition you don't have to hang about making a noise.'

The boys made a considerable detour so that they didn't have to pass Elspeth's house on the way home.

'You don't realise the worst,' said Alan. 'She's going to get in touch with Pam and collect signatures, too.'

'You're joking! You must be mad to give her Pam's name.'

'Well, if she wants to help, why shouldn't she? You and I happen to think she's a pain in the neck, but she's the type who'll do all the boring jobs for Pam. She's got no friends at school, and you never see her out with anyone. She's got nothing much in her life; she'll give all her time to SCAND—'

'And drive everyone mad in the process.'

'Pam said they needed people to go round sticking posters up. Dead boring. But I bet you the Weasel would do it.' Alan thought of those little feral eyes. 'But — oh, hell, Nick, why on earth did it have to be *her* house?'

When they returned the completed petition-sheets to Pam that evening, she was enthusiastic about their efforts.

'You've done as well as anyone. Now, what about joining a group of us next Saturday? I'm borrowing a minibus to take the petition round the villages between here and Maldham. It should be fun.'

They stared at her, tempted. 'The trouble is,' Alan explained, 'our exams are coming very close. We really can't take off too much time.'

'Forget it. Of course you mustn't. Just do what you can to get all your friends at school to sign. And, by the way, thanks for sending me that girlfriend of yours — what's her name, Ellen, Elspeth—'

'She's no girlfriend—'

'Whatever she is, I need more like her. Real eager types. I've given her Stagwell Quay to cover this weekend.' Pam lit a small cigar. She was taller than her husband, with strong shoulders and garage-mechanic hands ingrained with oil. She did the maintenance of the two taxis, while Jim took care of

69

the financial side. 'Go and see Robin Hawkes on Monday; he'll give you the petition-sheets for your classes.'

She started coughing over her cigar just as the phone began to ring. She waved the boys goodbye with streaming eyes.

'I've got the date when they're going to start drilling,' said Robin Hawkes the moment he saw the boys at school. 'I heard this morning. D-Day is the twenty-third of June. I had a look at the exam timetables and realised that you will have finished by then, which is a relief.'

'You can say that again.'

Hawkes put down his briefcase and got out sheets of the familiar petition-forms.

'Besides you two, who could I ask to help collect signatures? What about your sister, Alan?'

'She's not that interested.'

'What about Elspeth Riley?'

'People will sign anything just to make her go away.'

'Not kind, Nicholas Pope.'

'But true, sir.'

'She's already helping Pam Webb,' said Alan. 'She's dead keen.'

'And she's got a garden full of gnomes to protect her against radioactivity,' said Nick as Hawkes moved out of earshot. They saw Elspeth in the distance and hurried into the school well ahead of her.

'It's odd how some people bring out the worst in me,' said Nick. 'I've only got to think of the Weasel and I become mean as hell. See you in maths.'

Alan found it much harder to collect signatures in school than it had been on the Stagwell estate. Most people were apathetic.

'What's the point of signing? Nothing we do will change anything.'

Others were pro-nuclear. 'One accident doesn't change anything. I'm not prepared to do without heat and light in the future.'

Alan began by arguing, but people just drifted off rather than argue back. One boy, Chris Stillwell, told him to bugger off.

'I'm not signing anything. Get your name on one of those lists and it'll be fed into a computer somewhere and give you grief later on. I'm not signing.' He turned to his girlfriend, Janice Wilson. 'And don't you sign, either.'

'Fine. Please yourself.' Alan moved away, controlling a desire to sock Chris one. Five minutes later Janice tapped him on the shoulder.

'Give us the list, then. I may go out with Chris, but I'm not going to be told how to think. Pat wants to sign, too.' A girl who had hidden herself behind a pro-nuclear group added her name.

'You ain't got many from this class yet. What about the parallel?'

'Nick's covering that.'

'Tell you what,' said Janice. 'My big sister Kathy is very anti-nuclear. I'm sure she'd do the sixth form for you. She's not afraid to say what she thinks, either. C'm on. Let's go and find her.'

Janice dragged Alan to the sixth-form common room and, having asked for Kathy, left him to face her on his own. He waited nervously, and after five minutes decided to leave. She appeared as he turned to go. She fixed her extraordinary unblinking green eyes on Alan while he tried to explain about the petition. His tongue tied itself into knots. She gave him no help, and when he finished there was a pause before she said: 'Mr Hawkes is doing a petition, too.'

'This is all the same. We're on the committee of the same protest group in Stagwell.'

Kathy narrowed her eyes. 'I say, I say, on the committee. We *are* keen.'

'I'm not really on the committee.' Alan cursed himself for mentioning it. 'I just happen to be around at meetings.'

'A political agitator in the making, are we?'

'I'm not political.' Alan began to regret getting hold of Kathy Wilson, and backed off down the corridor. Suddenly she laughed, and her eyes stopped being sarcastic slits. 'If you want me to sign, I'll sign. But why don't you petition for actually shutting down the power station? I'd be really interested then.'

'This is a start. Talk to Mr Hawkes about the next stage.'

'I might.'

Alan took courage. 'Janice said you might be interested in collecting signatures in the sixth form.'

'Oh, she did, did she?'

'Forget it. I can ask someone else.'

'I didn't say I wouldn't.'

They stared at each other, testing out the ground.

'How old are you?' asked Kathy suddenly.

'Sixteen. Seventeen in September.'

'Is that Maddy Page your sister?'

'Yes.'

'You don't look like twins.'

'We're not. She's eleven months younger. Same class, that's all.'

'Ah.'

'She'll probably do better than me in the exams.'

'Don't you mind?'

'No.'

'Go on. Bet you do.'

'Not much. She works harder than I do. I'm not thicker, I'm lazier.'

'Give us a couple of sheets of that petition, then.' Kathy read the numbers at the side. 'Eleven hundred and upwards. Not bad.'

'We're hoping to get over twenty thousand.'

Bells rang all over the school. Kathy said, 'I'll be in touch,' as she disappeared. Her face stayed round the door for a moment, green eyes lively. Alan tried to think of something to say, but suddenly there was just a shut door.

SEVEN
Monday, 12 May

Green eyes. Alan wished he'd asked Kathy how old
she was. She could be nearly his own age: she was
only first-year sixth. She could be a couple of months
older than him, no more. Then the great divide
between fifth form and sixth form wouldn't matter
so much. He didn't ask himself why he cared. He
thought about Kathy Wilson all day, on and off.

'Did Kathy say she'd help?' asked Janice when they
next met, in the afternoon history period.

'Eventually.'

'She's a born tease, my sister. She scares all her
boyfriends off.'

'Oh, really?'

'Want a gum?'

'Thanks.'

'Old Foley is late. It's funny how some teachers give
up when you get near an exam, and others just get
frantic and try to pack a year's work into a month.'

'How old's Kathy?'

'Nearly seventeen.' Janice flicked another fruit gum into her mouth. 'Here's Foley. 'Nother gum?'

'No, thanks.'

When Alan got home he found the house silent. It was half-past four; usually his mother and Luke were home by this time. Then he remembered Luke had gone on a school outing to London; perhaps his mother had gone, too. Alan decided to go out and do some final sketches for his art project; he needed to practise landscapes.

He bicycled to the Saxon chapel and prowled round it, trying to find a good angle to draw. Beyond the chapel on the seaward side were marshes; the sea shone in the distance. The marshes, now a bird sanctuary, were covered with bright patches of spring flowers, and the sky above was lightly dotted with white puffs of cloud. There was a wooden shed on stilts near the chapel which Alan knew was a hide reserved for birdwatchers. He decided that if he perched himself on the steps of this lookout, he'd have a better view of the marshes and the sea.

He settled himself on the top step of the precarious wooden staircase and began to sketch in pencil. He used a variety of different-leaded pencils to achieve light and shade, softness and hardness. Alan was extremely good at pencil drawings; he didn't handle paint so well. He often found he ruined his drawings when he added colour. He sat enjoying himself in the sun, the sad cries of seabirds and the whine of the power station the only sounds he could hear.

He finished one sketch and started another, this time in charcoal. He brought out the stark simplicity of the little chapel, and managed to capture a flock of gulls that wheeled above it, using quick sharp charcoal strokes which squeaked as he did them. He was so involved with this sketch that he did not at first see the two people who were climbing out of the next hide a quarter of a mile away. Birds flew up in alarm, alerting Alan to their presence.

A man and a woman were walking towards him. The man was Paul Norrington, and the woman was his mother. They were holding hands and laughing together. They stopped, kissed briefly and walked on.

Alan knew that they were bound to see him when they reached the path that took them past the chapel. He had to escape; at present he was visible but not obvious. He felt for the handle of the door behind him; it should have been locked, but the last person to use it hadn't bothered. He pushed the door open, grabbing his sketching things; his pencils and charcoals fell through the wooden slats on to the grass below. At least he was out of sight now; he crouched below the level of the windows, his heart pounding. He heard them pass by; Angie laughed once, quietly and happily, at something Paul said. Then there was silence again, except for the birds and the whine.

Alan peered out to check, then sat down on the wooden floorboards of the hide and let loose his sense of shock. He didn't notice that his shoe was on his charcoal drawing, spoiling it.

Paul and Angie. Whatever they'd been doing up in that hide, he was sure it wasn't birdwatching. They weren't carrying binoculars and, besides, his mother hardly knew a gull from a pigeon. Paul Norrington. How could Angie like that awful creep? And let him touch her. . . . Alan felt sick.

'God, why did I have to come here today?' But he knew that not knowing what was going on wouldn't solve anything; if Paul and Angie were secretly meeting each other, one day someone would see them. Stagwell was a small place. They hadn't been particularly careful, holding hands like that in the open. . . . Alan banged his head against the wall. Just as well it was him and not some busybody who'd seen them.

Paul Norrington was married. Surely he wasn't going to divorce Elaine and marry Angie. This thought was so appalling Alan went quite rigid. It was the worst-case scenario, right in their family. He would move straight out if that man moved in.

Maddy and Luke — what would they do? Alan realised that in moving out he would be in a sense betraying them. But not as badly as Angie had betrayed all of them. . . . Alan sat for a long time in the hide. Light was beginning to fail; he was late for the evening meal. But he could not go home yet; he couldn't face his mother.

He stood up, and realised some of the pain inside him was pure hunger. He picked up his drawings and saw the smears of charcoal all over the top sketch. He rolled it viciously into a ball and threw it in a corner of the hide, where it joined a couple of empty beer cans. He went to his bicycle, wondering if his mother had seen it. He had tucked it well behind some brambles, so he thought it was unlikely.

He was poised at the top of the hill, in an agony of indecision. To the left was home; to the right Stagwell Quay and the Popes. He went right. The Popes would have eaten long ago, but Jean was always kind about allowing Nick's friends to raid the larder. He felt none of his usual exhilaration going down the hill, and pedalled unseeing past the marina. If the power station had disappeared, had sunk into the earth, he would not have noticed. As he turned into Nick's gate, he realised he had left his pencils and charcoals behind on the grass.

Nick was up in his bedroom, working. He looked surprised to see Alan, particularly as Alan flung himself immediately on to Nick's unmade bed and lay staring at the ceiling.

'What's up?'

'I was just sketching at the Saxon chapel—'

'Seen a ghost or something?'

'I saw Mum with a man.'

'So what?' Nick looked unimpressed. 'She's got to find herself a boyfriend some time.'

'But the man was that bastard Paul Norrington who works at the station. Worse, he's married.'

'Not so good.' Nick pushed his books aside and sat staring at his friend. 'What's got into her to fall for him, then? They were doing more than just walking along admiring the view, I take it?'

'They came out of one of the hides. They were holding hands. Paul kissed Mum a bit.' There was a pause while Nick flicked a textbook over and over.

'Well, you never know,' he said at last. 'They could be just passing the time.'

'I can't understand what she sees in him in the first place.'

Nick's blue eyes met his friend's. 'You'd probably think that about anyone she fell for. I often can't see what Ma sees in Dad.' He laughed, and Alan relaxed a little.

'Hell, I'm famished. I missed my meal this evening. I didn't want to go home.'

'You've picked a bad day — we're right out of food. We had a mixed load of rubbish for tea. Ma was moaning that we were even out of sugar.'

'Lend me some cash for fish and chips, then.'

'I'm stony broke. Why don't you go home? Bet your food's still in the oven.'

'I couldn't face Mum.'

'Yes, you could. Tell yourself it wasn't serious.' Nick yawned, and pulled his books towards him.

'Whatever you do, I've got to get on and finish this.'

The telephone rang downstairs, and Jean's voice shouted up. 'Nick? Is Alan there?'

'Yeah.'

'Angie wants to know what he's up to.'

Alan came to the top of the stairs. 'Tell her I'm on my way home.'

'She says she's got to go to a meeting at the school, so she won't see you till late.'

'Thanks, Jean.'

Alan cycled home feeling relieved he wouldn't have to face his mother for a while. He found Luke watching television, his hair wet and on end after a bath. Maddy was up in her room.

'Nick just rang.' Luke spoke with his eyes on the box, his lips barely moving.

'But I've just left him—'

'He rang.'

Torn between his agonising hunger and his curiosity, Alan grabbed a potato from the pan on the stove and dialled Nick's number while he stuffed it in his mouth.

'Nick.' Chunks of potato dropped into the receiver.

'I just wanted to say if I were you I wouldn't tell anyone else what we talked about.' Nick had to talk in a roundabout mutter because the only telephone in the house was audible to all.

'I'd like to tell Maddy.'

'Suit yourself. I wouldn't. If it turns out you've been making a mountain out of a molehill, you'll have got her worried for nothing. See you.'

Alan fished the pieces of potato out of the receiver and threw them in the sink. He felt touched that Nick had bothered to ring him and say what he thought, and in his heart knew his friend was right. There was a plate of stew keeping warm, and he plonked the cold potatoes and cauliflower on top of the hot meat and wolfed the lot in record time.

Up in his room, he looked across at the Norringtons' house. There were lights on everywhere, and few of the curtains were drawn. He saw that Paul was on a stepladder in an upstairs room, fixing something; beside him stood Elaine, passing up the tools he needed. It was a calm domestic scene, husband and wife happily busy together. Alan began to wonder whether he'd dreamt what he saw that afternoon.

He also realised he hadn't given a thought to Kathy Wilson for hours.

EIGHT
Friday, 16 May

'Kathy Wilson wants a word with you,' said Nick.
'She's down by the dispensers.'

Alan had looked out for Kathy all week without
catching a single sight of her. He rushed down the
stairs and found her screwing her face up over a
coffee.

'This coffee's terrible.'

'The soup's worse.'

'I need another petition-sheet. I've got going on
the upper sixth, and I've run out of space. Mr Hawkes
is not in this morning apparently.'

'There's some space on one of mine. I'll get it for
you. Hang on.'

'I'll come with you. I've got to go upstairs anyway.'

As they ran upstairs, Alan was aware that Kathy

81

only came up to his shoulder. A crowd of children rushed past them, pushing and shouting. Kathy stumbled and fell against Alan. For a moment he held her soft slim arms and smelt her newly washed hair. His heart was thudding.

'Do you mind?' he shouted after the noisy kids, more to cover his confusion than out of any real annoyance. Kathy swiftly detached herself, and they made their way to Alan's classroom in silence. She waited outside while he fetched two half-filled forms, one of Nick's as well as his own.

'Great. Thanks. See you.' She shot away.

'Are you coming to the meeting tonight?' Alan shouted after her.

'Of course.' Kathy's voice floated from the stairwell.

'I'm coming, too,' said Elspeth. He turned to find her watching him. 'I'm dying to hear what the up-to-date total of names is. Yesterday Pam told me we'd reached ten thousand.'

'Really.'

She blocked the way into the classroom. 'It's well above her target for the first week.'

'Great, but I must get my stuff. . . .' He managed to ease himself past Elspeth and saw Nick grinning at him.

'We've got six weeks to prepare ourselves.' Robin Hawkes stood on the platform in St George's Hall and looked round at the crowded room. 'First, the petition is being taken up to Downing Street on Wednesday. There's plenty of room on the coach, so anyone who'd like to go please tell Pam here.' Pam waved a list in the air. 'But our main aim is to organise, and publicise, an effective blockade. Fortunately, there's only one approach-road to Stagwell Mound, and the obvious place to build a barricade is just by Ollie Tanner's

82

garage. Ollie has agreed to let us use his forecourt for the scene of operations. We need to keep everything we use to block the road well off it until the last moment, otherwise we could be in trouble with the police for obstructing the highway! But as soon as we see the drilling convoy we fill the road with people and whatever constructions we decide to use. From the experience of other councils, the drilling convoy starts by being very polite; they give notice of precisely what hour they plan to arrive. They try diplomacy, and if that doesn't work they start taking the blockaders by surprise.

'Now, we already know that the first lorry will arrive at nine a.m. on Monday the twenty-third of June. We need to know roughly how many people we can rely on for help with the blockade and with all the publicity stunts we hope to organise. I suggest anyone interested in helping with the blockade comes and sees me, while those good at ideas for publicity go and see Ken, Nick and Alan down at the far end of the hall; and you, Pam, put yourself somewhere in the middle for volunteers for the coach.'

There was an immediate buzz of noise as people started moving from their seats. Alan looked around for Kathy, and at that moment saw her rush into the hall.

'What have I missed?' she asked. 'My moped's playing up, it took me ages to get it started.'

'Not a lot. Hawkes has just appealed for volunteers. Blockade, publicity, coach.' Alan pointed to the relevant corners.

'I'm going on that coach. Can't wait to get close to our dear Prime Minister.' Kathy joined the throng near Pam. 'Are you going?'

'I don't think I can. It's just before the exams.'

'I'll test you on the coach.'

A glow spread through Alan as he realised she was prepared to sit by him. To hell with it; he'd go.

There was bedlam round Pam Webb. A large fat woman was suggesting she should bring her three small kids, and Pam was trying to say no as politely as possible.

'You need some little kids; they're the ones that are going to suffer the pollution the most.'

'We've already got some coming. Too many and it looks like a playgroup.'

Alan grabbed a piece of paper and wrote on it: 'Definite for the coach: Kathy Wilson and Alan Page.' He pushed this in front of Pan and hissed: 'Book us in.' She waved a distraught hand as she continued her argument with the fat woman.

'You're not going on that coach, are you?' Nick looked annoyed. 'You're crazy.'

'I've changed my mind.'

'Hawkes said no one doing exams would get permission.'

'Kathy's going to test me on the coach.'

Nick's expression showed exactly what he thought of this idea. 'Tell Dad I'm off,' he said, and left the hall abruptly.

Kathy was already easing her way into the crowd round Hawkes. Her crash helmet sat on a chair near Alan; he noticed she had stuck a small black and white CND badge on to the back as if it was part of the trim.

'Alan!' Ken shouted from the end of the hall. 'Where's Nick? You boys are supposed to be giving me a hand.'

'What do you want me to do?'

'Take down this lady's details, would you?'

'Fine.' A woman with short grey hair and colourful messy clothes smiled at him.

'My name's Sophy Robertson, 23 Estuary Road,

telephone 74789. I used to be a scene painter. I'll paint anything for you.'

As Alan wrote all this down on a pad, a thought struck him. 'We need a long piece of fabric to hang from a hot-air balloon. It should be really eyecatching — have a slogan painted on it that can be read for miles.'

Sophy Robertson laughed. 'A hot-air balloon. What a good idea. Leave the banner to me; that sort of thing is just up my street. How long do you need it?'

'Twenty feet?' Alan expected her to be taken aback. Instead she said: 'Are you sure that's long enough? You want it to be easily seen and read from the ground. I would have thought fifty feet would be more like it. Bright yellow.'

'Ken? What do you think of a fifty-foot yellow banner hanging from Winter's balloon?'

'Wonderful! Can you really do that for us?'

'No problem. I've still got access to cheap fabrics. Don't worry about the cost anyway. I'll donate the banner to the cause. Give me ten days to make it.'

'That's the kind of help we need,' said Ken later, taking the pad from Alan and looking at the names he'd scrawled on it. 'And the chap who's a carpenter is going to very useful. I've asked him to come to the farm on Sunday afternoon, so that we can get going on my specials. Two-thirty, Alan. Don't forget.'

Alan nodded, but felt a cold cramplike feeling in his stomach. Everybody was asking for his time. He ought in fact to go home right now and get on with his revision. Maddy would be bent over her books, so by now would Nick. He turned to go, and was tapped on the shoulder. Kathy grinned at him, swinging her helmet.

'What about a cup of coffee somewhere, before I leap on to my untrusty steed?'

'There's only Joe's open at this time of night. It's a dump, too.'

'Where's Joe's?'

'At the end of the High Street. It's a pizzeria and coffee bar. I'll go ahead on my bike and show you.'

'OK.' She tucked her head into her helmet and did her chinstrap up. The helmet had an odd effect: by disguising her face completely, it drew attention to her extraordinary green eyes. Framed by the globule of red, they flashed at Alan, coolly humorous. She followed Alan through Stagwell, unhealthy smoke pouring from her exhaust.

Except for a couple of people finishing their pizzas, Joe's was empty. As they sat down in a corner, Alan suddenly realised he had no money.

'Damn.'

'What's the matter?'

'I've left my money at home. I'll just go and get it. I'll be back in five minutes.'

'Don't be silly, Alan. I'll stand you a coffee; you can buy me one another time.' Kathy sat down at a table and called out to Joe for two coffees. 'I'm really glad Nirex have decided to try to dump waste at Stagwell.'

'I don't follow.'

'Because it will wake people up to the nuclear threat. People are so apathetic. Everyone says: "Oh, it can't happen here." Bet they said it at Chernobyl.'

'They say it everywhere.'

'Do you have nightmares?'

'Yes.'

'I get them, too. And I get driven crazy by people saying there's nothing we can do, the world has had it, so let's put our heads in the sand and enjoy what we've got while we've got it. My family is as bad as that lot — except for Janice; they say I'm exaggerating, they say we need nuclear power and nuclear weapons, they say all the risks are in a good cause. Even after Chernobyl, they're still convinced mankind has to learn from its accidents, so accidents have to happen.'

'Which could be true—'

'Yes, but, Alan, mankind hasn't got *time* to learn from its accidents. All we can learn from Chernobyl is that if one of our own power stations explodes we've had it. England's too small and too crowded to isolate the disaster area the way they're doing at Chernobyl. Stagwell goes up and *bam*! London's affected.'

'I know. You don't have to persuade me, Kathy. I agree with every word you say.'

'Sorry. I tend to bang on about it because so many people I talk to don't seem to see the truth of what I'm saying.' Joe put down the two cups of coffee in front of them, and Kathy paid him, telling him to keep the change as she handed him a pound coin. 'Mind you, I'm not sure SCAND agrees with me, either.'

'What do you mean?'

'I told Robin Hawkes that protesting against the dumping of waste wasn't enough; what we should be pressing for is the closure of the power station. He more or less shut me up. First things first, he said, giving me a no-go-area look. Then someone else said Stagwell's quarrel wasn't with the power station with its excellent safety record, but with waste-dumping systems that are untried. I was about to argue, but Hawkes was huffing and puffing at me so I beat it.'

'Quite a few people in SCAND are pro the station and anti the dump.'

'I see. Listen, do you happen to have a cigarette? I forgot mine.'

'I don't smoke.'

'I hardly do, but sitting talking over a coffee always makes me want a fag. Smoking's stupid, I know, but I do lots of stupid things.' She sipped her coffee and laughed slightly. 'My dad says it's crazy to worry about things like radiation and then poison my body with cigarette smoke. I have a good answer for that one.' Her eyes were full of triumph. 'It's *my choice* whether I pollute myself with nicotine and get cancer; it is *not* my choice if a power station blows up or a nuclear warhead goes off — and I get cancer from radiation.'

'What did he say to that?'

'I think he saw my point. For once.' There was a pause. The other people had gone, and Joe was wiping surfaces and putting things away. Kathy's hand lay beside Alan's; he wanted to touch it. Perhaps she'd come to the cinema with him; then he could hold it in the dark—

'But to get back to the protest group — SCAND or whatever you call it. It does seem a bit mad to me to make a fuss about the waste when there's a couple of real live nuclear reactors getting old and unreliable actually on your doorstep.'

Alan wished Kathy would get off the nuclear subject sometimes; she tended to return to it at every opportunity. It was hard to say 'Can you come to the cinema?' when she was talking about Magnox reactors.

'After all, they were only built to last twenty-five years—'

'I'm closing now, kids.' Joe gazed at them morosely; he was an elderly Italian whose aim in life was clearly not fulfilled by this grotty café in rural Essex.

'Have you been waiting for us? Sorry, sorry. We were talking so much we didn't notice.' She collected her denim jacket and her helmet and smiled at Joe as they left. His gloomy expression eased up briefly in reply. They heard him bolting the doors as they stood on the pavement.

'Thanks for the coffee.' Alan was expecting to stand about talking for a while longer, but Kathy moved her moped off its stand, started it first kick, and with a wave of her hand was gone. He had never met anyone who said goodbye and disappeared so quickly. Disappointed, he biked home to face hours of revision. His mother called to him as he crept through the house.

'Alan? You're late.'

'The meeting went on a bit.'

'Come in here when you've put your bike away.'

Angie had her spoiling-for-a-row expression on. She wore half-moon reading-glasses, and if she didn't take these off her children knew that she was angry about something.

'This is ridiculous, Alan.'

'What's ridiculous?'

'All this protest action just before your exams. You'll fail them if you're not careful.'

'I'm keeping up with my work.'

'Alan, don't give me that. You can't be. Revision takes time as well as concentration. Time is something you've been wasting recently.'

'I'm getting more done than you think.'

'That wouldn't be difficult.'

'Listen, Mum, the protest group is important. It's not my fault everything's happening right now.'

'Your protest group is not going to change a thing, however hard it tries. Nirex is going to march in just the same and drill holes and put radioactive stuff in them, if they decide the spot is suitable. They own the land, and in the long run they'll win.' Angie took her glasses off and rubbed the bridge of her nose. 'I really feel the whole protest is a waste of time. It's making me very angry that you're letting it affect your schoolwork.'

'I'm not sure I'd have worked any harder if I'd had more time.' He stared at his mother, resentment growing in him. 'Look, you're not being fair. Why shouldn't people be angry about a nuclear-waste dump?'

'I think half the folk are protesting because they get a kick out of it.'

'That's better than not caring at all. You don't care, Mum, do you? You seem to be in favour of unlimited nuclear power.'

'Alan, that's quite untrue.'

'Well, what is your position, then?'

Angie met his eyes for a second, then turned away. 'We can't undo the fact we've got nuclear fission. So we must harness it and live with it as safely and constructively as possible.'

'But that's just it! "Safely and constructively"! What does that bloody mean?'

Angie leant back in her chair and closed her eyes. 'I'm getting tired of the nuclear debate.'

Alan felt even more annoyed with her. 'That's not going to make it go away. Only closing down the power stations will make this particular nuclear debate go away.'

'But you can't just close them down. Think of all the people round here who work at the station; they'd lose their jobs.'

'Like your darling Paul.'

Angie lay very still. Then she opened her eyes again. 'Why call him that?'

Alan felt like someone who was about to dive off a rock into water that might turn out to be too shallow. He dived anyway.

'I saw you and Paul together down on the marshes.'

'I go for a walk occasionally with Paul. He's a good friend to me.' Angie spoke extra-calmly to try to hide her agitation. 'It may have escaped your

attention, but Paul and Elaine are the first new friends
I've made in a long time.'

'You and Paul were holding hands. He kissed you.'

'It didn't mean anything. I know it must have
looked bad, but deep down it didn't mean anything.
And I won't go out alone with him again, I promise.'

Angie gazed directly at Alan. She didn't look the
least bit guilty, just upset. He had to believe her,
and ninety per cent of him did believe her.

'Were you afraid of us becoming serious about
each other?'

'Sort of.'

'You needn't worry. I've seen the danger, I really
have.' She stood up and put an arm round Alan. 'I
don't want to spoil my life with the three of you,
you know that.'

Alan could not take any more of the charged
emotional atmosphere. 'I must go and do some work.'

'Good idea. Don't stay up too late. And promise
me you won't let this protest business interfere too
much with your revision. It's not worth it.'

'No, Mum.'

DEATH SENTENCE

Two old women have been found hiding in their farm in the deserted countryside near Chernobyl. Irina, 70 years old, and her sister Katya, 68, said they would rather die from radiation at home than be evacuated to spend the rest of their lives in a strange place.

But they were given no choice. Both were taken to the refugee centre near Kiev. . . .

Daily News

NINE
Wednesday, 21 May

'Say yes!' said Kathy. 'Tell him you'd love to see round it as soon as possible and can you bring some friends — then I can come, too.'

'They'll spend half their time trying to persuade us that the power station is absolutely safe—'

'Always listen to the enemy viewpoint.' Kathy drained her tea and threw her polystyrene cup into the wire basket nearby. As usual, the area around the dispensers was crowded with people. Alan often wondered why the authorities didn't make the lobby less lavatorial, since it was the school's main meeting-place. 'It'll be great to see inside the station. I've always wanted to.'

'Next time I see him, I'll fix it up. He lives right opposite us.'

'See you at the coach.' Kathy disappeared with her usual speed. She was the only person Alan knew who left a gap in the air when she'd gone.

'Hi.' Nick joined him on the stairs. Ever since Kathy's arrival on the scene, Nick had been cool.

'Hi. How's life?'

'OK. What happened about your mum, by the way?'

'My mum?'

'And that man Norrington.'

'You were right. She says there's nothing in it. We talked about it the other night. The night of the meeting, in fact.' Alan realised how little he'd seen of Nick since then. Normally they'd talk at length every day.

'I'm glad. I thought your reactions might have been over the top.'

'I hope she's telling the truth. People kid themselves.'

'Alan, you have to accept what she says. Stop worrying.'

'I'm not worrying.'

When they reached the next floor, Nick said in an undertone: 'You're not still going on that coach, are you?'

'I'm playing it by ear.'

'Have you got permission?'

'I haven't asked.'

'I did, and the Head refused me. I'm just warning you. Nobody with exams about to start is allowed to go.'

'If I go, I'll do it without permission.'

'Hawkes will see you. He's on the coach.'

'By then it will be too late.'

'You're crazy.'

The coach was collecting supporters from various meeting-points in and around Stagwell and Maldham. Anyone going from the school was asked to be in the market-place by noon. As the time approached, Alan began to dither. There was a special maths revision class that afternoon which he'd be a fool to miss. He tried to see Kathy, but was told she'd already left. He'd have to go. She expected him to go, and also expected to test him.

'I'll give you such a tough time you'll be sorry you came. I'm a demon tester.'

Alan packed a heap of books into a carrier bag and let himself out of the staff entrance — strictly out of bounds to pupils, but it was the only exit that didn't give on to the playground. He hurried to the market-place, and saw Kathy, with another first-year sixth, Sue Dempster, and a boy from the year below Alan. Kathy waved. Alan felt some of his apprehension melt.

'Got all your books?' said Kathy.

Alan held up his bag. 'You'll regret this.'

'Not as much as you'd regret not doing it.'

'Hawkes might stop me going.'

'Here it comes,' said Sue Dempster, pointing to a coach waiting at the lights on the other side of the square. They could see NO DUMPING written up where the destination of the coach was usually put. The sides of the coach were plastered with signs: STAGWELL SAYS NO TO NUCLEAR WASTE — ANY DOSE OF RADIATION IS AN OVERDOSE — NO TO NIREX! The nuclear logo transformed into a skull and crossbones decorated any spare inch that didn't have a sign. Even the wheelhubs had a skull stuck firmly to each.

The coach was attracting attention all down the street. When it stopped to pick up Maldham supporters, two reporters promptly leapt out of a parked car and started talking to Robin Hawkes. This gave Alan the opportunity to slip on to the coach unnoticed; he and Kathy installed themselves near the back on the off side, and Alan kept his head down until Maldham was behind them.

'Welcome to the new arrivals,' said Hawkes over the intercom. 'We've only got the supporters at Palworthy to pick up now, and then it's straight to London.' The whole coach cheered. Kathy giggled.

'It's like a school outing. Any minute people are going to start singing. OK, Alan, get the books out.'

'Oh, come on, Kathy, not yet.'

'Yes. If we don't get going at once, we won't at all. Anyway, quick, Mr Hawkes is coming down the coach. He'll be less annoyed if you're working.'

Out came Alan's French grammar, and Kathy went straight into reflexive verbs. By the time Hawkes got to them, they were sorting out the past tense of *s'asseoir*.

'It's *je m'assis*. Hullo, Mr Hawkes. The bus looks great.'

'Hullo, Kathy, Alan. Alan.' Hawkes stopped in his tracks. 'You're not supposed to be here. Exam candidates were expressly forbidden to come.'

Alan and Hawkes gazed at each other.

'I'm going to revise all the way there. And back.'

'The Head is going to be very angry about this.'

The Head is not going to know, hoped Alan. He tried to grin at Hawkes. 'I couldn't miss this.'

'Look, Mr Hawkes, we've already started work. I promise I'm going to test Alan until the stuff comes out of his ears. And if we have a problem with the physics' — she smiled brilliantly — 'please may we come and ask you?'

'You're a pair of devils.' The coach pulled on to dual carriageway, and began hurtling towards the Palworthy turn-off. 'I could turf you out and make you hitch-hike back.' He was frowning, but not very convincingly.

'He'd waste more time getting back to school than he would sitting here in the coach.' Kathy's eyes were wide and innocent.

'I know I shouldn't have come,' began Alan.

'But you're here now, and I'm going to have to lump it. OK. But this isn't the end of the matter, Alan Page. I'll have to report you to the Head. He was adamant that none of your year came.'

'Shit,' said Kathy, as Hawkes went back down the coach. 'I think he means it.'

'I'm sure he does.'

'I'll work on him.' Kathy sighed. 'On with the French.'

'No, leave it to me. The best thing is if he sees us slogging away.'

So they slogged away during the drive to London: French, history, geography. Kathy had strong powers of concentration, and never flagged as she pored through Alan's notebooks picking out what he needed to revise.

'Stop, stop,' begged Alan at last. 'I'm going to explode. Anyway, we're in the City already. We'll be there soon.'

The coach parked on the Embankment, underneath a canopy of thickly leaved plane trees. Big Ben shone, newly cleaned, against a bright blue sky; tourists were everywhere, taking photographs of the Houses of Parliament, of Westminster Bridge with Boadicea in her chariot forever galloping towards Parliament.

A man stood selling silver heart-shaped balloons; a little boy had let his go, and it sailed up into the sky, hovering high over the Thames. One of the Stagwell mothers went and bought half a dozen balloons for the children on the coach; on each balloon was promptly stuck a label bearing a nuclear skull and crossbones. Robin Hawkes and Pam Webb started pulling protest banners out of the hold.

'Here, Alan. You and Kathy take this one. And you, Sue, carry one of these.' Hawkes handed over a floppy white effigy about three feet high with a nuclear-skull face. A dozen of these were handed round, all of different sizes. The biggest was man-sized, and had a skeleton painted on it as well as the usual skull. 'The plan is to dump these "bodies" in a heap outside Number Ten.'

Alan and Kathy unrolled their banner. It said in uneven, red capitals: WE DON'T WANT A NUCLEAR FUTURE.

'Poor execution, good message. Up it goes!' said Kathy.

With much laughter and joking, the fifty or so protesters got into a crocodile and started to walk towards Parliament Square. They had a small police escort, and various reporters joined them as they marched, asking questions up and down the line. Alan and Kathy were asked some fairly fatuous questions by a girl from LBC.

'Are you enjoying the day off school?'

'It would be great if I didn't have exams looming,' said Alan, while Kathy leant forward and cut in: 'Anyway, coming is a duty not a pleasure.'

The LBC reporter's smile did not quite reach her eyes as she went on: 'Alan and Kathy are carrying a banner which says WE DON'T WANT A NUCLEAR FUTURE. Could you tell our listeners a little more about your views? Kathy?'

'The banner sums up my view.' Kathy spoke crisply. 'I say stop the arms race and close the nuclear power stations. That's why I've come on this demo. Stopping the dumping is just a beginning.'

'And you, Alan?'

'I think mankind's got to turn back the scientific clock for the first time in history. We've got to forget we know anything about nuclear fission.'

'Do you believe that's really possible?'

'Anything's possible.'

The interviewer moved on, and Kathy said: 'That sounded very impressive.'

'It was the first thing that came into my head. Load of bollocks probably.'

'Hey, my arms are aching already. How the hell are we going to keep this up high for another hour?'

'Try tucking the end into your jeans pocket.'

'We *are* full of bright ideas today.'

The crocodile shambled slowly across the lights at the end of Westminster Bridge, and went round to the front of the Houses of Parliament. Several be-skulled balloons had escaped — one danced its way up to the face of Big Ben, and then caught on a pinnacle above it. A cheer went up from the pavement.

'Well done, little Sarah!' But Sarah wailed dismally at the loss of her balloon, and would not stop until her mother bought her another.

By this time a crowd of press, reporters and photographers, were collecting round them. Robin Hawkes and Pam and Jim Webb tried to tie a banner to the railings of Parliament, but were stopped by the police. They were also told they couldn't tie an effigy to the railings as they'd planned to. Disappointed, the group started off again towards Whitehall.

It was at this moment Kathy suddenly said to Sue Dempster: 'Hold my end of the banner, would you, and give me that.' She grabbed Sue's ghoulish white figure and darted towards the tall elaborate railings. Before the police could stop her, she had jumped up and flung the effigy so that it landed plumb on the spike of a railing, neatly impaled. The skull leered down, the limbs hung pathetically. Loud cheers came from the increasing crowd, and dozens of cameras clicked to record the oddly disturbing sight. Kathy was nowhere to be seen: she had darted immediately into the thickest part of the crowd, and was keeping her head down.

Leaving a couple of policemen trying to remove the effigy — they pulled its legs off first — the Stagwell demo marched away, greatly encouraged by this little victory. Kathy eventually reappeared at Alan's side, looking very pleased with herself. She took the banner from Sue and winked at Alan.

'Let's hope a photo of that makes the front pages.'

'It was brilliant, Kathy.'

Hawkes came to find Kathy. 'Well done. But keep a low profile now — we don't want you being arrested.'

'I wouldn't mind. It's all publicity. Why don't we all lie down in Downing Street? With a name like that, it's asking for it.'

'Because I don't think it would achieve anything. Please, Kathy, no more colourful gestures. You've done your bit.' He smiled and moved on.

'Some hopes,' said Alan.

Kathy was looking rebellious. 'Why is it all teachers are wet blankets, even the nice ones?'

They marched on for a while in silence. Then Sue Dempster, who had been scouting ahead, came back and told them that there were television crews waiting in Whitehall near the entrance to Downing Street.

'There's masses of police there, too. You'd think we were a really big demo.'

'Instead of three men and a dog from the sticks.' Kathy was still disgruntled, but she looked more cheerful when she saw that among the television crews was a very well-known reporter.

'Well, if they send her, they must think we're important. Despite appearances.'

There were metal barricades across the mouth of Downing Street, and these apparently were not going to be moved. Only two people were allowed to deliver the petition. Groans of disappointment went through the group.

'What a farce,' said Kathy. 'I thought we'd be able to get close to the Prime Minister. It's the main reason I came.'

The petition was handed over and Hawkes and Pam Webb were back in minutes. One of the Prime Minister's secretaries had taken it off them with assurances it would go straight to the PM's office.

'Oh, yeah. I can see her regarding it as riveting reading. It'll sink without a trace. We've got to make people pay attention by doing tougher things than getting together petitions.' Kathy grumbled away at Alan, who half-agreed with her. Nor were they allowed to leave the effigies anywhere near Downing Street.

'They might contain bombs,' hissed Kathy darkly.

'We ought to leave them somewhere. It's stupid to take them back to the coach.' Alan and Kathy dropped to the back of the rather dispirited group of demonstrators.

'There's nothing to be done. We can use them again later.' Hawkes spoke with finality. 'Don't let's waste them; they took a lot of making.'

'Feeble,' muttered Kathy.

They wound their way back to Parliament Square, until the galloping chariot of Boadicea was opposite them. Kathy and Alan nudged each other. They both gazed at the splendid statue.

'Are you thinking what I'm thinking?'

'Yes. Hold this,' said Alan to Sue, giving her his

100

pole. He went down the column and within minutes was back with a particularly gruesome white effigy of a child. He took his end of the pole back from Sue, who moved away, suspecting that the two of them were up to something.

'We'll dash across together and put the sign and this thing as high on the chariot as we can,' Alan muttered to Kathy.

By this time they were behind the rest of the column. As the others went down the Embankment, Alan and Kathy grabbed the opportunity of a red light and ran across to the end of Westminster Bridge. Boadicea and her chariot were on a high granite plinth, but conveniently beside it were two solid municipal rubbish-bins. Kathy and Alan used them to climb on to the plinth, then they propped the two poles into the bodywork of the chariot, so that the ancient British queen galloped into battle with the legend beneath her that she didn't want a nuclear future.

By this time most of the protestors from Stagwell had stopped, and were staring across the wide busy Embankment at what was happening. Hawkes was waving angrily. Some people were cheering. A lone policeman was worriedly talking into his radio.

Alan climbed higher and hung the effigy on to Boadicea's spear, ramming it well on.

'Quick, Alan, jump down.' Kathy was already on the pavement. 'Quick, let's split before the police get here.'

As Alan leapt down, the balloon-seller who had watched the whole episode with delight, said: 'That's given the old girl a bit of excitement. She always looks so fed-up—'

'Poor old bag—'

'Quick, Alan, police!'

The two of them started to run down the river side of the Embankment. Their luck was in; a crowd of at least fifty American tourists were wandering along towards Westminster, filling the pavement. Kathy and Alan melted into them and kept out of sight until they were more or less opposite their coach. Most people were now inside it; the banners and effigies were being stowed away. Sue Dempster was still out, staring worriedly back towards Westminster Bridge. A couple of policemen were hurrying towards the coach.

'Don't cross yet, keep walking.' Alan took Kathy's arm, and they strolled on and then pretended to gaze into the Thames below them, their elbows on the Embankment wall.

'Mr Hawkes is obviously telling the police he hasn't a clue where we are. He looks furious.'

'Let's walk on a bit more.' Tensely, they strolled beyond another group of tourists, Germans this time, all busy with cameras.

'They haven't seen us. Sue has got back into the coach.'

Alan looked quickly round again. 'The police have pushed off.'

'No, hang on, let's make sure. The coach won't leave without us.'

But it did. To their horror, the doors hissed shut and it started to move. Alan and Kathy rushed to the edge of the pavement and waved frantically. Then they saw Hawkes making pointing directions, and realised he was telling them to move on down the Embankment. A couple of hundred yards further on the coach stopped, and Alan and Kathy rushed across and leapt on to it. A roar of cheering and clapping went up from everyone; Hawkes alone looked furious. Pam was trying to be severe, but failing.

'Go and sit down. I'll come and talk to you in a minute,' growled Hawkes. 'For God's sake don't encourage them,' he shouted down the coach, to no avail. 'They're lunatics. Behaviour like that could discredit our cause.'

But everyone was winking and whispering 'Well done!' They sank into their seats at the back, out of breath. Kathy immediately reached into Alan's bag and pulled out a book. It happened to be *Macbeth*.

'Right. Testing, testing. Here's a context—'

'Give us a chance, Kathy. My brain's in a bloody whirl.'

Kathy took no notice.

' "Foul whisperings are abroad. Unnatural deeds
Do breed unnatural troubles; infected minds
To their deaf pillows will discharge their secrets." '

She hissed this dramatically at him.

'You're a hard unfeeling woman. Just like Lady Macbeth.'

'Well, where's it from?'

' "Foul whisperings" — that's her, isn't it?'

'You're supposed to tell me.'

'Oh, God, Kathy, do I have to?'

'Yes.'

'I've no idea where it comes from, no idea.'

'It's the Doctor, after he's been listening to Lady Macbeth when she's gone bonkers.'

'You mean, after the "Out damned spot" bit—'

'This is very commendable, but it's not going to save a row.' Mr Hawkes stood beside them. 'I'd be grateful if you'd let me have your place for a while, Sue, while I talk to this pair.'

There was a pause; Kathy did not close up the

103

copy of *Macbeth*, and kept running its pages through her fingers.

'I expressly forbade you, Kathy, to take any more action after your first colourful effort.'

'Oh, come on, Mr Hawkes, we didn't do any damage.'

'It's a free country, sir.' Alan spoke as quietly as he could. He knew Hawkes liked people to be reasonable. 'We weren't on school business, either.'

There was another pause. 'What you're saying is that I haven't, in terms of this demo, got any control over what you do.'

'That's about it, sir.'

'He's right,' began Kathy.

'Even if he is right,' interrupted Mr Hawkes, 'which I concede he might be, there's the question of the wisdom — or total lack of it in my opinion — of what you did.'

'We made the public see our point.'

'What public? The police will have pulled down your stuff within minutes; a few cars, a few buses that were passing will have seen your great gesture, and that's it. You were just doing it for kicks. What annoys me is that it makes SCAND look like a half-baked organisation run by kids, only interested in making eyecatching but meaningless gestures.' His tone was scathing.

After an even longer pause, Kathy muttered: 'Well, it was fun. And the balloon-seller won't forget us.'

'I don't see why something run by kids has to be half-baked . . .,' began Alan.

'OK, that was uncalled for. I'm sorry. I'm being a bit hard on you both, I know, but it's been a hell of a day to organise, and I admit I'm disappointed by our reception at Downing Street. I expected

104

something more positive to happen.' He rubbed his hands over his face. 'I should have known better.'

'There'll be lots of publicity.'

'We hope. A few minutes on the national news could make the whole trip worthwhile.'

When Hawkes had returned to his seat, Kathy whispered: 'Actually, I think he's jealous. He'd love to have done something flashy himself.'

'You're probably right.'

They both stared at the back of Hawkes's head and felt sorry for him.

'It must be murder getting old,' said Kathy. 'On which point:

> "Tomorrow, and tomorrow, and tomorrow
> Creeps in this petty pace from day to day
> To the last syllable of recorded time." '

Alan did not have to think. 'Macbeth himself. Act five, scene five. Just after Lady Macbeth's death at Dunsinane.'

'Alpha double plus.'

SOVIET LEADER ADMITS RISING DEATH TOLL
The death toll, originally given as 2, has now risen
to 9. A further 300 people are in hospital with varying
degrees of radiation sickness.

Doctors are dismayed by the complex and unexpected range of radiation-induced conditions. 20
victims have received bone marrow transplants,
others have developed severe liver, kidney and lung
failure, which makes any operation futile.

The Daily Telegraph

TEN
Thursday, 22 May

The publicity exceeded everyone's wildest hopes. All
the national networks gave the Stagwell demonstration
full coverage, mainly because it was the first against
nuclear-waste dumping to reach Downing Street with
a petition. Luke watched goggle-eyed all evening,
shouting for Alan whenever the demo appeared in a
news bulletin. Alan's great sentence about mankind
turning back the clock — which he had repeated
several times to various reporters — was used by the
BBC to sum up the whole occasion, and there was
Alan himself in close-up, looking cool. Luke gazed
at his brother in utter admiration.

'Don't be fooled, Luke. It's a load of cobblers.
They just ask you one question, and if you give a
zippy reply they show it. Kathy Wilson said much
more interesting things than I did.'

Luke took no notice. 'I'll be able to tell them at school you were on telly, and that'll shut Michael Scobie up. His sister was on "Blockbusters" and he went on and on about it.'

Alan found himself briefly famous, and so did Kathy. A photo of her impaling the effigy on the railings outside the Houses of Parliament appeared on the front of five national newspapers. Only *The Times* did not show her; instead its picture was of a policeman pulling the leg off the effigy as he tried to get it from the spike.

Alan and Kathy managed to meet briefly at the lunch break. 'It's amazing what publicity will do for one's image,' said Kathy. 'All these friends I didn't know I had.'

'You're only real if you appear in the media, didn't you know? Until then you don't exist.' Alan fended off a third-form admirer.

'I'm just sorry that the press missed the decorating of Boadicea.'

'I'm not. Mr Ellershaw wants to see me. I had a note from him first thing. The less he knows the better.'

'I see your point. Look, I must go. See you.'

Alan needed more moral support than that for his looming interview with the Head, so he looked for Nick. Nick had been avoiding him in school, nor had he been in the bus that morning. Alan found him in the library. Since they were alone, Alan sat on the table and broke the silence rule.

'Missed you this morning. How did you get in?'

'Dad had an early appointment, so he brought me.' There was a pause, then Nick went on: 'Sounds as if yesterday went well.'

'The press make it seem a lot more exciting than it really was. In fact it was dead flat most of the time.

107

If Kathy hadn't stuck that effigy on the railings, the whole demo could have passed unnoticed by everyone except the police. We weren't even allowed into Downing Street. Kathy and I got so annoyed we stuck a banner and another effigy on to that statue at the end of Westminster Bridge. Old Hawkes was livid.'

'With all this publicity the Head's going to find out you went.'

'He has already. I've got to go and see him in ten minutes.'

'Not good.'

'Not good.' Alan went to the window. The youngest classes were filing back into school after the lunch break. 'I suppose he could expel me.'

'Go on, Alan, not just for that.'

'I've got a bad feeling about it.'

'He couldn't, not just before the exams.'

'He's a cold bugger. I've got to go.'

'See you on the bus this evening. Don't let the bastards grind you down.'

Mr Ellershaw had what he called the Headmaster's Surgery for an hour every day from one till two. This was supposed to be used by pupils needing help and advice, but because he was a brusque and unsmiling man, nobody went to see him of their own accord. The hour was therefore filled by pupils summoned for breaking the rules or not working. In front of Alan was a boy famous for two facts: that he never did any homework, and that he was one of thirteen children.

Alan saw him go in, and sat waiting on a window-sill staring at his grubby trainers. After a while he took his French grammar book out of his pocket and tried unsuccessfully to learn some vocabulary.

Footsteps came up beside him, and a hand touched his shoulder.

'Alan.' Elspeth Riley leant towards him. 'I had to come and say how marvellous I thought you were on telly yesterday.' Her whisper was piercing. She gave off her usual feral niff. 'It doesn't matter what happens in there' — her eyes slid towards the dreaded door — 'as long as you remember it was all in aid of the cause.'

'Look, Elspeth, I'll get in even worse trouble if Ellershaw comes out and finds me talking. Push off.'

'I just had to tell you—'

'Thanks, but *push off*—' There were sounds of movement from the Head's study. Elspeth scurried off. The door opened.

'Right. Your turn, Alan Page. Come in and sit down.'

Mr Ellershaw's study was unexpectedly friendly and comfortable. ('KGB tactics,' said Nick. 'Making sure you feel at ease before you're tortured.') The Head always made pupils sit in the armchairs rather than on the upright chairs opposite his desk. He waved Alan to a large chintz-covered chair and himself sat on the arm of another.

'That was a very interesting day you all had in London yesterday.'

'Yes, sir.'

'I even heard you regaling the nation with words of wisdom on the news.'

'Yes, sir. Sorry about that—'

'You have more than that to be sorry about. I take it you were aware I had expressly forbidden all exam candidates to join Mr Hawkes's demonstration.'

'Sort of, sir—'

'Ten pence.'

'Ten . . .' Alan wondered if Ellershaw was mad.

'I exact a ten pence fine every time anyone says sort of. There's the box. If you haven't got the money now, tomorrow will do. If I were you, I should avoid really great, shouldn't of, off of, you know, and several others you'll find listed on the fines box. It can get expensive.' He pointed to a collection box bearing a label headed: LINGUISTIC ABOMINATIONS. Alan solemnly fished 10p out of his pocket and dropped it into the box. As he did so, the Head said:

'I am tempted to expel you.'

Alan went cold.

'If you didn't have exams looming, I wouldn't hesitate. I am tired of the way you and others like you use the school as you please, and take no notice of rules and embargoes.'

Alan watched the Head's mouth saying embargoes — not that he knew what it meant — and hated him.

'This school seems to possess increasing numbers of anarchists—'

'I'm not an anarchist, sir.' Alan often found that taking an unexpected point threw an angry teacher off balance. As usual, it worked.

'You behaved like an anarchist. You took no notice of my ruling.'

'But I thought you were right to forbid us to go to London. Anarchists would question that. I don't. Sir.' Alan definitely felt he had won that rally.

'Then, why did you go, if you held that view?'

'Because I thought it was more important to support SCAND than it was to obey school rules.'

'Don't tell me that your presence on that coach trip made any difference to the protest at all,' spat out Ellershaw. He obviously thought he'd won that point, and Alan felt it was wiser not to disagree; the less the Head knew about the publicity caused by him and Kathy the better.

'They needed supporters,' he said lamely.

'Perhaps they do, but that's not the point. You can hold what views you like, but when they start interfering with your school life, then I step in.' Mr Ellershaw glared at him. Suddenly Alan was past caring.

'Look, sir, it's not my fault that Nirex have chosen the same time as our exams to put pressure on Stagwell.' He stood up. 'It's not my bloody fault. But it's the first time in my life I've cared about an issue beyond my little world, and I'm *glad* I went.' He was shaking, and expected to be expelled then and there.

Mr Ellershaw stared blankly at him, frowning. Then he walked over to the window and started to tap on the glass. At last he turned round and said: 'Oddly enough, I respect that. Yes, I respect that.'

Alan was so surprised he sat down again.

'However, the next time you want to take prohibited action, and you think you have a good reason, come and discuss it with me first. You never know, I might have let you go.'

'You didn't let Nick Pope go, sir.'

'He didn't put up such a good argument as you have.' There was a knock on the door. Ellershaw called, 'One minute,' and went over to his desk.

'Rather to my own surprise, and no doubt to yours, I've decided not to punish you. Just this once — and I mean just this once. Now, let the next person in, will you?'

'Yes, sir.' Alan stood up but did not move. 'Thank you, sir. I'd say you'd been sort of really great, you know, but I can't afford to.'

'Get out before I change my mind.'

When Alan got home from school that day his mother was lying in wait for him. She had been out the

111

evening before, and Alan was hoping by some fluke she might not have heard about his exploits in London.

'Alan.'

She'd heard.

'Yes, Mum.'

'Come here. Everyone in Stagwell but me seems to know what a hero my son is.'

'The press exaggerate everything—'

'Alan, I'm disappointed in you. Really disappointed. You promised me you'd give up all this stupid demonstrating and work for your exams. The next thing I know you've played truant and you're waving banners in London.'

'I revised in the coach all the way there and all the way back.'

'Don't give me that, Alan. Nobody can work in a coach full of chatting people.'

'Well, I did. Kathy never let me stop.'

There was a pause while Angie poured herself more tea. 'And who is this Kathy who also seems to have caught the public eye? I've never heard you mention her before.'

'She's the sister of one of the girls in my class. She's well into CND and stuff. That's why she came.'

'Maddy said she was trouble.'

'It's none of Maddy's business and, anyway, she doesn't know what she's talking about.'

'Maybe. But I know what I'm talking about, and I say if you fail those exams you retake the lot of them. I'm not having a son of mine leaving school without the minimum qualifications.'

The phone rang, and Alan picked up the receiver. It was Pam Webb, saying that a reporter wanted to interview him.

'This isn't a very good moment, Pam—'

'If that's Pam Webb, tell her you're not doing any more protesting—'

'He'd just like five minutes, Alan—'

'Don't you commit yourself to anything, Alan Page.' Angie was reaching out for the receiver.

'Look, Pam, I'll ring you back.'

'It's now or never; he's off back to London soon. He's from *The Times*, Alan; I wish you'd see him.'

'OK, send him round, but explain I'm tied up with revision and stuff.'

'So what was all that about? I won't open the door if it's someone coming to waste more of your time.'

'Pam said only five minutes. It's a reporter from London.'

'I don't care if he's from outer space. Five minutes is all he'll get. I'll time him.'

Alan ran upstairs to escape his mother and to take off his uniform. He had only just got into a T-shirt and jeans when he heard the doorbell go. He moved fast, but his mother moved faster and got to the door first.

'His exams start next week.'

'I promise you I'll waste very little of his time, Mrs Page.' The man on the doorstep had a light pleasant voice, and was wearing a smart suit. He was smiling at Angie, who was visibly relenting. 'I'm writing an in-depth survey of everyone's attitudes to the threat of a nuclear-waste dump at Stagwell, and I would love to talk to your son because he's been unusually active.'

' "Unusually" sums it up. Come in, anyway. Tea?'

'No, thanks. I don't want to put you to any trouble.'

'The pot's made.'

'In that case. . . .'

Alan lead his visitor into the front room, while Angie went off to the kitchen.

'I'm Reginald South, of *The Times*. Do you mind if I use this recorder?'

113

'Go ahead.'

South took a small sophisticated machine out of his briefcase, and started asking Alan the usual questions, but with a slight twist to them. He also watched Alan very closely.

'How would you feel if this anti-dumping protest were a stepping-stone to the closing down of the power station itself?'

'I'd be pleased. I admit it didn't occur to me when I first got involved, though.'

'What changed your attitude?'

'Chernobyl. Other people. There are some very keen talkers involved in SCAND.' Alan grinned at Reginald South. 'You ought to interview one of them — she's a teenager, too.'

'Here in Stagwell?'

'No, in Maldham.'

'I'm sticking to Stagwell this time.' South took a cup of tea from Angie. 'Thank you so much, Mrs Page. I've nearly finished with Alan. One final question. What does the presence of the power station mean to you in your everyday life?'

'It means that awful noise. *Eeeeeeee.*' They all stopped to listen.

'It doesn't bother me,' said Angie.

'It's always got on my nerves. If I'm tired or fed up, I notice it particularly. I've never got used to it.'

'You're exaggerating as usual, Alan.'

'I am not. I just don't mention it much. What's the point? It's always bloody there.'

Reginald South switched off his recorder, looking quietly pleased. He finished his tea while talking politely to Angie.

'I'm not sure when this article is coming out, unfortunately. Do you get *The Times*?'

'No.'

'Well, I'll personally make sure we send you a copy.'

'I'm sure he doesn't do that for everyone,' said Angie after South had gone.

'Bet he does. They have to be sharp about sweetening people up. Plus we might switch to *The Times*.'

'You're a cynic.'

'I'd rather be a cynic than a dupe.'

Alan worked all evening, and then decided at about ten-thirty that he needed to talk to Kathy. His call got a cool reception from Mrs Wilson, who said, 'I'll see if she's gone to bed,' in the tones of someone who felt the whole world should be asleep by ten at latest.

'Hi.' Kathy sounded far from sleepy.

'Have I got you out of bed?'

'You must be joking. So what's the problem?'

'No problem. I just rang for a chat.'

'What's new, then?'

'Not much. Gave an interview to *The Times* today.'

'Why you in particular?' Kathy was edgy.

'He was doing a survey of Stagwell opinions. I was the specimen teenager.'

'What about Maldham's opinions?'

'Not interested at the moment. I tried to put him on to you.'

'I'm fed up with all this publicity anyway.' Pause. Kathy yawned audibly. Alan wanted to keep her talking, but couldn't think of much to say.

'Everyone's mad with me for going to London.'

'More fool them.' She didn't ask how the session with the Head had gone.

'I'm glad I went. It was one of the best things I've ever done.'

'What a deprived life you've led, Alan Page.'

'Come on, Kathy, you enjoyed it, too.' In his

mind's eye he could see her expression of exhilaration and triumph as she rammed the effigy on the Parliament railings.

'Yeah, well, it was OK.' She yawned again. 'I'm waiting for some real action. Look, I must go.'

'Hang on, Kathy, I wanted to ask you when we could meet or go out or something—'

'See you at the barricades against Nirex. I'm really looking forward to that. Must go, Alan. And good luck with those exams.'

Alan went back to his room and stared sightlessly at his textbooks. He picked one up and put it down. Kathy. Kathy. It was clear she didn't want to see him outside the protest set-up. She didn't like him for himself, just for the fact that he thought like she did. This realisation made him feel thoroughly depressed. He wondered if he had fallen in love.

He started to go downstairs to make a cup of coffee but he saw his mother in the kitchen and couldn't handle her right now. He went up to Maddy's room. She was lying on the floor in a bodysuit, swinging her legs about.

'What are those things strapped to your legs?'

'Weights. They make all exercises even more effective. Sally lent them to me.'

'They haven't had much effect on Sally.'

'She's too lazy to do the exercises in the first place.' Maddy sat up and unstrapped the weights. She then put a measuring-tape round her thigh, 'Not that I can see much difference, either.' Gloomily, she put the tape round her waist. Her expression changed. 'Hey, I've lost an inch! Well, a bit less than an inch but more than half an inch. That's great.'

Alan flung himself on Maddy's bed. 'Girls make me sick.'

'Look, it's my body, and if I want to get it into shape that's my affair.'

Alan began to feel that perhaps confiding in Maddy about Kathy was a bad idea. He'd come up longing to talk about her, but he could regret it later. So instead he said: 'How's the revision going?'

Maddy pointed to a chart on her pinboard. She'd listed all the revision areas in great detail; most lines were ticked or crossed off.

'A tick means I've sort of covered the topic; when it's crossed off I'm really on top.'

'Old Ellershaw would fine you ten pence.'

'For revising? You're joking.'

'He had this list of things you mustn't say — he calls them Linguistic Abominations. Like "sort of". Say them in his study and he fines you.'

Maddy said reflectively: 'Do you know, I've never been inside his study.'

'That's because you're a hardworking prig.'

'Belt up.'

Alan pointed to Maddy's revision chart. 'It's true, Maddy. Look at that. I bet no one else in England is as organised as you are. It's unreal.'

'The trouble is, I'm ambitious.' Maddy put on a large shirt and sat on the carpet. The back of her short-cut ginger head was very neat, very determined. 'I want to do really well. Everyone at school thinks it's smart not to work. I think they're stupid. Work is the only thing that makes school interesting as far as I'm concerned. No wonder they're all bored out of their minds, mucking about doing nothing the whole time.'

'You needn't overdo it, Maddy. Everyone calls you a swot and a goody-goody.'

'I really don't give a damn.' Maddy lay flat on the carpet and shut her eyes. 'You're a bit of a swot yourself compared with some of the others.'

'I've caught it from you. And I've got another bone to pick with you, Maddy.'

'Oh, yes?'

'Will you lay off Kathy?'

'Lay off Kathy?' Alan was aware Maddy was watching him from her seemingly shut-eyed position on the carpet.

'I don't know why you've got this down on her.'

'Down on her? I hadn't noticed I'd got a down on her.'

Maddy was smiling to herself. Alan felt like whamming a pillow on to her face.

'Mum said you'd been giving her a bad press.'

'Oh, tut, tut.'

'Belt up, Maddy. You hardly know Kathy. Stop making trouble.'

'We *are* touchy all of a sudden. Is Kathy Wilson so important to us, then?'

This time Alan let fly with the pillow. Maddy fended it off, and the pillow rose high and flopped against the mantelpiece. There was a nasty sound of breaking glass.

'Oh, bloody hell, Alan. Look what you've done.' Maddy kept a fleet of small glass animals on her mantelpiece. They looked as if a cyclone had hit them. Maddy stared red-faced at the wreckage.

'Sorry, Mad. You shouldn't have lifted your arm.'

'They're nearly all broken.'

'Sorry. But you did say the other day you were fed up with them and were going to give them away—'

Maddy turned angrily on him. 'I decided not to, if you'd like to know. I realised they meant quite a lot to me.'

She picked a pink glass horse with broken legs from the mess. 'Gran gave me this when I was six.'

Her face was screwed up, almost like a six-year-old's about to wail. Alan got up.

'Look, I said I was sorry. I'll buy you some more if that's what you really want.'

'Get out, Alan. I'm fed up with your patronising attitude—'

'Hey, Maddy—'

'Just because you're going out with a sixth former, you don't need to do the older-brother act over me—'

'I am *not* going out with Kathy Wilson.' Though I wish to hell I was. Alan suddenly felt as tearful over Kathy as Maddy had been over her glass animals. There was a pause, during which Maddy dropped the shattered remains into her tin wastepaper-bin.

'Tinkle, crash.' Maddy let go a headless giraffe. 'There goes my childhood.' A dog and a nameless feline beast followed into the bin. Soon the mantel-piece was empty.

'I'd like to go out with Kathy, but she's not interested.'

Maddy appeared to take no notice. 'This one's still whole.' She held up the pink and yellow glass object in her hand. 'It's hideous, isn't it?' She dropped it from a height into the bin where it shattered noisily. 'Actually, to be honest, Alan, I don't mind those things getting broken really. I'd had enough of them.' She smiled at him, an oddly sweet smile. 'So thanks for getting rid of them.'

'Any time.'

'You're dead lucky Kathy isn't interested in you. From what Janice tells me, she eats men for breakfast.'

MINERS IN DANGEROUS STRUGGLE

More than a month after the disaster, 400 brave coal miners quarry under the stricken reactor in order to build a giant concrete cooling slab.

Because of the lethal radiation levels, the miners are being driven to and from the tunnel in specially protected armoured troop carriers. All wear respirators nicknamed 'petals' to prevent them inhaling radioactive dust from the sandstone in which they are digging. Temperatures in this 'dragon's lair' are dangerously high. . . .

The Herald

ELEVEN
Tuesday, 10 June

The classroom clock seemed to leap from midday to twenty past. Every time Alan looked up it was as if someone had deliberately moved the hands on. A fly was crawling up the glass case heading for three o'clock. He dragged his eyes back to his paper, and looked at his last words: 'Macbeth is frightened of Lady Macbeth. He becomes almost like a hen-pecked husband in the course of the play. . . .' Hell, was that true? He added another couple of sentences, beginning to feel that it wasn't. But it was too late to change the direction of his answer, because suddenly the teacher invigilating said: 'Two minutes.' Alan read through the last page he had written and muttered to himself: 'What a load of balls.'

'No talking. Who spoke?'

No one took any notice. Everyone was frantically rustling sheets of paper. Alan saw out of the corner of his eye that Maddy had written reams. He collected his sheets together and felt satisfied that at least he had managed to finish all the questions, even if the last was rubbish. He headed out of the room towards his maths books, taking no notice of anyone. All round him people were starting to do a post-mortem on the paper. He hated discussing exams once they were over. Besides, the worst ordeal of the entire week lay ahead of him that afternoon, and he'd decided to eat his packed lunch alone somewhere and mug up formulas. As he was collecting his books Nick joined him.

'Shitty paper.'

'Yeah.' Alan was poised to leave. Nick looked miserable. 'It's this afternoon I'm dreading.'

'Me, too. Are you eating in the canteen?'

'No. I'm off to find a quiet corner, and do a year's maths in an hour.'

'See you later.'

'Let's take a crate of beer out in the boat after we've finished the exams, and get pissed while we fish all day.'

'Great idea.' Alan grinned at his friend. 'The moment they're over.'

'Can't wait.'

As he headed towards the unpopular and mucky area behind the gymnasium, he ran into Kathy.

'Hi, Alan, long time no see. Actually I wanted to talk to you—'

'I can't stop. I've got things to do.' He could see by the playground clock he had only three-quarters of an hour left.

121

'This is important. I've had an idea for the barricades and I need your reaction—'

'Look, I've got maths in half an hour. Ring me tonight.' Alan hurried away; he couldn't help feeling pleased that for once he was taking the initiative. He settled himself down on a large crate that had been lying for months behind the gym, and gobbled his sandwiches while flicking through his maths book.

The trouble was there was nothing he could do at this stage, and he knew it. His maths was very patchy, and if he was unlucky he'd certainly fail. He'd probably fail anyway. He lay back and stared up at the sky through the trees above him. It was hot and muggy, and the sky was almost colourless. He continued to stare, losing himself in patterns of leaves against the sky. The playground din receded, and he felt strangely calm. Time passed without his realising it; a hand on his shoulder made him jump up startled. It was Nick.

'So this is the way you revise maths.'

'When the situation's hopeless, the best thing is to relax.' Alan's lunch-tin fell to the ground, and they kicked it along between them as they went back into the school. Alan's sense of calm continued even when he opened the dreaded exam paper. He worked his way steadily through all the questions he could manage, quite enjoying himself. He was going to fail, so he might as well go down cheerfully. He finished all he could do half an hour early, and saw that most of the class who were bad at maths had also stopped writing. But Maddy, next to him, had also finished and was double-checking her pages. This made Alan look again through his paper, and he corrected several slips. Then he began to wonder whether there was just the faintest chance he might have passed.

He and Nick played backgammon in the bus home and by mutual consent did not discuss the maths paper.

'How did the maths go?' asked Angie. She was busy making a steak and kidney pie. She believed in feeding people heartily when they were doing exams, whatever the temperature outside. Sweat beaded on her forehead.

'I liked it.' Maddy put ice in her drink and went into the hot garden.

'I survived.' The phone rang, and Angie picked it up with a floury hand. It was Guy Winter, for Alan.

'Feel like a ride in a balloon?'

'Wow. Yes.'

'We're flying over as much of Essex as possible next Sunday, trailing the banner. There's space for one more person, and I thought of you.'

'Next weekend.' Alan could see his mother's ears twitching. 'I've still got some exams the following week—'

'It's only for a few hours. Come on, Alan. If you've never been up, grab the chance. My father's going to sell the thing soon.'

'Don't you agree to anything next weekend,' whispered Angie, poking the rolling-pin at him.

'Honestly, Guy, it's really impossible. If only it was the weekend after that.'

'That's too near the arrival of the Nirex drilling team. It's got to be this weekend to get the right publicity. We're taking a TV camera up with us. Go on, you must come.'

'I'll try—'

'Whatever all this is about, don't agree to anything,' hissed Angie.

'Look, Guy, I'll ring you back when the situation's clearer—'

'Get your work organised and come.'

'I'll come if I possibly can.'

As Alan put down the receiver, Angie exploded. 'You're not doing anything next weekend, Alan Page. No demos, no delivering pamphlets, no nothing. I forbid you, and that's final.'

Alan went out into the garden rather than argue. Maddy whispered: 'What was that about?'

'Guy has asked me to go up in their hot-air balloon.'

'Lucky thing.'

'Lucky hell. Mum says I can't go.'

They could hear Angie slapping pastry about, and then the crash of the oven door as she put the pie in to cook. She came out into the garden, her face red from the heat in the kitchen, a streak of flour on her cheek. She announced crossly to Alan: 'All right. I leave it to your conscience. If you think you've done enough work, and you're satisfied that you're fully prepared for the exams you've got left next week, then you go. But I warn you, Alan, if you fail those exams I'll be furious.'

'I'll never get another chance to go up in a balloon. They're selling it after this.'

'Put going up in a balloon against the prospect of retaking your exams, and I think you'll agree it's not worth it.'

'I'll probably have to retake them anyway.'

The phone rang, and Maddy got there first. She waved the receiver at Alan. 'It's Kathy,' she said, making a face of exaggerated surprise. Alan took the phone, consigning both his mother and his sister to temporary extermination.

'Hi, Mr Hard-to-find, got you at last. I've already rung twice. Didn't your mother tell you?'

'No.'

'Listen, you know you said you had a contact in the power station?'

'Yes.'

'Well, fix up that visit he promised.'

'I'm going to.'

'Great. Get us in soon, Alan — before the twenty-third of June when the drilling starts. See if we can go round after school hours, or on a Saturday.' As Kathy chatted enthusiastically, Alan felt hunted. Everyone was doing their best to wreck his exams.

'Listen, Kathy, my exams don't finish until the twentieth. That's a Friday. The blockade is being set up that weekend; we'll be needed. There's no way I can fix it before.'

'It's important, Alan. I've had a brilliant idea. But I have to get into that power station. Haven't you got a free day in between your exams?'

'Tuesday's free, but—'

Alan was suddenly aware that his mother was standing by his shoulder.

'Give me that phone.'

'Just a minute, Mum—'

'Please give it to me. I want a word with this Kathy.'

'Mum, please go away.' Alan had his hand over the receiver. He could hear Kathy rattling on about stunts and publicity. 'I can handle my own life.' He hung on to the receiver. Angie picked up a large pair of kitchen scissors.

'I'll sever the line if you don't let me talk to that girl.' Alan knew she meant it. Sometimes his mother went crazy. He handed over the phone.

'Hullo, Kathy, this is Alan's mother.' Angie's voice had gone suspiciously sweet and reasonable. 'I'd like to ask you to leave my son alone until his exams are finished. Ten days more, that's all.' Kathy's voice started to speak, but Angie continued: 'When they're over you can pester him as much as you like. But not before. 'I'm sure you'll co-operate, won't you?' She put down the phone.

'You had no business to talk to her like that.'

'I'm fed up with all your friends distracting you.'

'Kathy doesn't pester me. There was no need to use a word like that. No bloody need at all.' Alan went out of the kitchen. 'I'm going out, *with* my work. I'm going to Nick's to revise. Don't worry, I won't let him pester me.'

'Wait a minute, Alan, there's no need to over-react. . . .'

Alan carried on upstairs. He was shaking with anger.

'I interfered for your own good,' called Angie after him. She threw down the scissors, and raised her hands to her face.

'Leave it, Mum.' Maddy started to follow Alan.

'This Nirex business is beginning to drive me mad.'

'Take no notice of it.' Maddy stood by the door, picking at a loose flake of paint.

'Do you think I was wrong talking to Kathy like that?'

'You should have let him sort it out for himself.'

'I did it partly because you said Kathy was a bad influence—'

'Don't give me that rubbish, Mum. I never said anything as strong as that.'

'Well, you implied it.'

'You heard what you wanted to hear.'

'What do you mean?'

'Just that.' Maddy started to go towards the stairs, watched by her mother. Then Alan came down with a knapsack full of books and went out of the front door. He didn't slam it, though he looked as if he was going to.

'I made the steak and kidney pie mainly for him.' Angie stood miserably in the middle of the kitchen.

'Freeze it for another time. I'm not hungry anyway.'

Luke appeared from the living-room. 'I am. Can we have Baked Alaska soon?'

'How I hate teenagers,' muttered Angie. She took a can of lager from the fridge. 'They drive anyone to drink. Ungrateful, insensitive toads.'

'Urk urk urk,' croaked Maddy, and went up to her room.

'So when can we have Baked Alaska, Mum?'

'I'm sorry about my mum, Kathy.'

'She certainly was charming. Careful, don't let her hear you talking to corrupt little me—'

'I'm ringing you from Nick Pope's.'

'So she's driven you out of the happy home.'

'I'm revising with Nick.'

'You'd better ring off quickly, then. Think of the things you could be learning while you're talking to me.'

'No, wait, Kathy. Don't be upset because of Mum's choice of words.'

'It doesn't matter. I'm not particularly upset by her. I'm more annoyed with you.'

'Me?'

'It's really important we should get into the power station before we start the blockade. They might never let us near the place once we begin demonstrating for real. You're the person who's actually had an invitation to see over the place, and now you're being wet about it. I expected you to have it all set up straight after your last exam, but no, all I get from you is excuses.'

127

There was a silence after this tirade of Kathy's. Then Alan took a deep breath.

'Leave it to me. If it's possible, I'll fix it.'

'There you go again. If. If.'

'I'll fix it.'

Then Alan phoned Guy.

'I've had a think, and I've decided to come on this balloon trip.'

'Great.'

'But, Guy, can I ask you a big favour?'

'Go ahead.'

'If by any chance I run out of time and start panicking, would you take a friend of mine instead of me?'

'Sure thing, if they're keen on the demo.'

'She's keener than any of us.'

'I thought you'd be suggesting Nick Pope.'

'He's got the same problem as me.'

'So he has.'

'Kathy Wilson hasn't got exams; she's in the year above us at school. She's a real live wire.' Alan smiled to himself. The old cliché was a good description of Kathy. You certainly got plenty of shocks from her.

'Fine. I'd rather you came yourself of course, but we'll take her up if you can't come. She's not the nervous sort, is she?'

'Not Kathy. She'd stroll around inside a lion's den.'

'She isn't the girl who decorated old Boadicea with you, by any chance?'

'That's her.'

'Well, well. I've heard a lot about her. It'll be interesting meeting her at last.'

Alan felt unaccountably uneasy at this remark of Guy's, and wondered whether suggesting Kathy for the balloon trip was a wise move. He went back into the Popes' dismal parlour, and tried to bury himself in his revision. But he couldn't concentrate, so he began to write a letter to Paul Norrington.

Dear Paul,
I've been thinking about your offer to show us round the power station, and now that my exams are nearly over, I wonder if we could fix something up? The afternoon of Friday, 20 June would be good, or the Saturday. I'd especially like to hear your side of things before the anti-dumping demo starts, so that I can have a chance to change my mind.

Yours
ALAN PAGE

PS. I know Maddy wants to come, and there's also a friend called Kathy Wilson who's interested. I hope that's all right.

This letter took Alan five drafts; he finished it finally before going to sleep that night, after he'd crept into the house at about midnight. He was quite pleased with the final result, particularly the bit about changing his mind. He'd have to make sure Maddy didn't come, though. The combination of her and Kathy would be too much.

Alan pushed his letter through Paul's letterbox as he left for school, dislodging the newspaper that was half in, half out. He heard it plop inside as he hurried away. It was just as well he didn't realise then that the newspaper lying under his letter was *The Times*, containing a long article by Reginald South on the inhabitants of Stagwell.

THE FEAR AT TMI
It was a dark and rainy day, March 30, 1979. Jean
Trimmer went on her front porch to look for her cat.
As she leaned over the railing, she says she suddenly
felt the strong wind stop dead and a wave of heat
engulf her. Then the gust of heat brought the rain over
her, and the wind began again. She went inside and
washed, but her skin began to feel tingly. Then she
noticed that her arms and face were pink. . . . Tiny
hard lumps developed on her forehead and along her
hair line. . . . Her hair started to fall out. . . .

'They say if you wash right after being exposed
to radiation, you can wash it off. When I came in that
day I did wash my face and hands, but not until after
I'd wiped the cat. . . I didn't know. . . . I was so dumb,
so dumb. . . .'

Philadelphia (American magazine)

TWELVE
Wednesday, 11 June

'In the news again, I see.' Mr Hawkes had invigilated
that morning's exam, and caught Alan as he went out.

'News, sir?'

'I didn't realise Reginald South had interviewed
you as well.'

'Pam sent him along. He only stayed ten minutes.'

'He's given you quite a lot of space.'

'I haven't seen the article.'

'I've got it in the staff room. Follow me and I'll

show it to you.'

There was a roar of noise as Hawkes opened the staff room door; sounds of someone singing 'Happy Birthday'. Hawkes shut the door behind him as he fetched *The Times*. 'Pop it back into my locker at the end of the lunch break. I shan't have time to read it now — we're celebrating Miss Temple's birthday.' Miss Temple was a popular, rather giggly teacher of PE. Alan wandered off, his eyes fixed on South's article, which took up half the features page. There was a dramatic photograph of Stagwell Mound taken through the masts of the nearby marina, and another picture of Ken Pope standing by the famous sign in his fields.

The article said nothing new, but summarised the whole situation vividly and without exaggeration. Alan read quickly until he came to his own name, then nervousness made him put the paper aside until he'd eaten his packed lunch.

Teenagers are usually apathetic about political or environmental issues, but in Stagwell I met some interesting exceptions. Mr Pope's son Nick, and Nick's friend Alan Page, both 16-year-olds, are very much interested in SCAND. Alan even risked serious repercussions at school by taking an illicit day off to go to Downing Street with the petition. He has already been quoted extensively in the media for his remark that mankind must turn back the scientific clock for the first time in history. I asked him if he thought it was really possible to undo scientific progress; to jettison nuclear development consciously and permanently.

'I don't see there's any choice. I know all the good arguments against it, but in the end all they're saying is that material comfort is more important than life.'

*I asked him whether he'd be prepared to accept
colder houses, fewer appliances, all the inconveniences
caused by a shortfall of power.*

*'Yes, I would. There's no choice. Otherwise the
monster in our midst will destroy us all one day.'*

*As well as unusual depth of involvement in the
world around him, Alan Page has a felicitous turn
of phrase. . . .*

Cobblers, muttered Alan to himself, but he couldn't
help grinning. He'd heard the phrase 'monster in our
midst' on a radio programme. He rolled up the paper
and put it in Hawkes's pigeonhole without showing
it to anyone. He felt ready to die of embarrassment
over these stupid catchphrases he seemed to use the
moment he was being interviewed by the media.

He found Nick collecting a coffee from the dispensers, and got himself a tea. They sat on a bench
in the sun.

'Dad's apoplectic about the latest Nirex move.'

'What's that?'

'They've leased the old sweetshop in the town and
called it the Nirex Information Centre or some rubbish
like that. It opened today. Full of pamphlets about
the wonders of nuclear power and the perfect safety
of all its waste. Nobody knew what the shop was until
they actually took the boards off.'

'The old sweetshop by Boots?'

'That's right.'

'Bugger them.'

'Dad was all for driving a tractor straight through
the plate-glass windows, but we persuaded him that
was a bit drastic. Instead, he's had a dead good idea.
Come down right after school; we'll show you. It
won't take long, I promise.'

132

*   *   *

In the back of Ken Pope's old truck was a large
rubbish-bin painted yellow. On it, very crudely
executed, were the skull and crossbones logo and the
words NUCLEAR WASTE. When Alan arrived, Pam
Webb was standing beside the truck, arguing furiously
with Ken; Nick was skulking behind the truck trying
not to laugh.

'I just think you shouldn't make publicity protests
without consulting the other members of SCAND
committee.'

'Bloody hell, woman, don't you think this is a
good idea?'

'I think it's brilliant, but that's not the point.'

'If it's a good idea, use it, that's what I say.' Ken
banged his hand on the side of his truck, and pieces
of rusty metal fell off.

Pam made a great effort to keep her cool. 'A good
idea used at the right time and in the right way
becomes even better. For instance, doing it today is
too soon.'

'Why?'

'Because the whole of Stagwell hasn't registered
the existence of the Nirex shop yet. And today is
Wednesday, half-day closing, so there won't be many
people around. Saturday morning would be better.'

Ken stared at her, unwillingly seeing the sense of
her words.

'What's the plan?' whispered Alan to Nick behind
the truck.

'Dad wants to put the dustbin outside the Nirex
shop, and then we all go in and out collecting pamphlets and dumping them all in the bin. But Pam's
right — we need lots of people to do it, not just you
and me and Dad! We need the press around as well,
if possible. Pam's winning.'

Pam and Ken were going off in the direction of the kitchen, to drink tea and telephone the rest of the committee.

'I think we could make a better job of this bin. Dad did it in such a hurry that it's a real mess.'

'You're right there.' Alan peered inside the bin. 'It's still got pigswill everywhere.'

'Dad said that was fit comment on the future contents.'

They wandered into the kitchen, scattering the chickens who always waited hopefully near the back door. Pam came from the phone briskly rubbing her hands. 'That's fixed — the dustbin demo will be on Saturday week. Midday. Get everyone you know to collect a bundle of pamphlets, and we'll have the bin ready right in the middle of the High Street. But try to keep it serious — a gang of giggling kids could make the whole thing misfire. Mark is going to make sure that the press is there. By the way, he says that the national media have booked all the available rooms in Stagwell that weekend, so they'll be around looking for action. He's going to prepare press sheets for them, giving details and timings of all events. I told him not to give those out too soon. We don't want Nirex as well briefed as the press!'

'They know everything already,' said Ken gloomily, a little put out that his dustbin demo seemed to have been taken over by Pam. 'All the locals who work at the Mound pass the info back for sure.'

'You're probably right. See you, everyone.' Pam drove off at speed. She tended to ignore SAFE SPEED IS YOUR NEED when she felt like it.

'I'd better get back. Slog, slog, slog. Roll on, Friday week,' Alan groaned.

'The hardest thing is having to work with all this activity going on the whole time.'

'You can say that again.'

Alan bicycled off. The twin reactors of Stagwell Mound hummed loudly; the late afternoon sun made its grey walls look invitingly golden. The monster in our midst, said Alan to himself. It didn't look like a monster. But it still sounded like one.

Suddenly, a car hooted behind him. There was Paul Norrington, leaning his elbow out of a new Rover. The sweet caramelly smell of unused car upholstery wafted out. 'Hullo, Alan. Thanks for your note. I'm glad you got in touch. That Friday is a bit difficult, though. I could get you shown round earlier that week—'

'I've got my exams until the morning of the twentieth of June.'

'That's the Friday. I see. Well, I'll work on it.' He smiled his overdone smile.

'It's not that important.'

'I disagree. I think it's very important for someone like you, an articulate teenager, with a felicitous turn of phrase' — he winked as he quoted this — 'to learn firsthand about the other side of the nuclear debate.'

Another car passed, and Alan nearly scraped against Paul's shiny new paint as he took avoiding action.

'Sorry.'

'No harm done. One of my fellow-workers going too fast.'

There was a pause.

'Is that noise louder when you're inside the reactor?'

'Not really. One gets used to it.' Alan and Paul stared at each other. Then Paul revved the car slightly.

'I'll be in touch about the precise date and timing, but let's hope it can be that Friday. I'll persuade one of the guides to give you a special tour. Goodbye, Alan, must be off.'

As Alan bicycled home in the evening heat, the whine of the power station seemed to follow him, getting louder all the time. He was very tired; perhaps that was why. For whatever reason, the sound went round and round inside his skull, invading his whole brain.

'Are you going ballooning on Sunday or not?' Angie tried to be casual. She handed him a can of iced Coke, a sure sign of bribery.

'Could be. Just get off my back, Mum, would you?' He took his aching head upstairs.

CHERNOBYL DEATHS RISE

Deaths from the disaster have now risen to 25, with a further 30 people in critical condition. The figure nobody knows is how many people will die of cancers in the years to come.

Russians have been told that the widely held belief that garlic and alcohol are a protection against radiation is a myth. . . .

The Guardian

THIRTEEN
Friday, 13 June

By Friday morning, Alan knew that he couldn't go on the balloon trip. Guy had told him to come at ten o'clock and had warned him that since the weather report was good the balloon might be up for most of the day. Alan could spare a couple of hours, but not the whole of Sunday.

Cursing the unfairness of life, he lay in wait for Kathy near the sixth-form common room. When she appeared Alan hardly recognised her. Her hair was scraped off her face and gelled back; she was wearing skin-tight leggings and a red cotton vest. She looked thinner; like a dancer. Alan realised he had only seen her swathed in layers before.

'Have a good look, won't you? It's a free country.'

'Sorry, Kathy. You seem different—'

'When it's as hot as this, even Kathy Wilson strips off a few clothes.'

'My pen keeps slipping in my fingers in the exams—'

'I can't think why we have national exams in flaming June. But you can't have been lurking by that door just to gossip about the weather. . . .'

'Kathy, would you like to go up in a hot-air balloon?'

He had surprised her; he had really surprised her.

'They're going to do a publicity stunt for SCAND with the Winters' balloon on Sunday, and Guy asked me to go along for the ride.' Kathy gazed at him, her bright green eyes eager but unhelpful. 'I want to go, I really want to go, but I just can't. I've got too much revision to do. I'd just sit there and worry. Guy doesn't mind if a friend goes in my place. I warned him I mightn't be able to come.'

'They're trailing a long banner, aren't they?' Kathy tried to sound casual and detached, but Alan could tell she was excited. 'Yeah, I'll go. I'm just a girl who can't say no to a hot-air balloon.' She grinned at Alan. 'Thanks, anyway. I'm sorry you can't go, but I'm pleased as well, if you see what I mean. What's this Guy Winter like?'

'Nice.'

'Naice?'

'No, he *is* nice; he's not all that Sloaney.'

'Who else is going?'

'Quite a few, but I don't know exactly how many the basket holds.'

'*Basket*,' squeaked Kathy. 'That sounds dead unsafe.'

'Apparently it's the best material for the job. Plastic cracks, metal's too heavy and reacts too much to temperature. Wicker's perfect.'

'Most baskets of my acquaintance have rapidly fallen to bits. I don't fancy falling a thousand feet.'

'Do you want me to see if I can find someone else, then?' Alan started looking down the corridor as if to find another person.

'No, no, don't be stupid. Of course I'll go. Even if the idea of sitting in a basket high above the earth sounds suicidal. Never mind. Think what a crash would do for the cause. Where do I meet them, and when?'

'I'll get the gen from Guy this evening.' Kathy was called back into the common room, and Alan wandered aimlessly towards the Middle School library. He felt very depressed.

Unusually, Maddy sat by him in the school bus.

'Where's Nick?'

'Gone to the dentist.'

'You look fed up.'

'I am.'

'Mum keeps asking me whether you're going up in that balloon on Sunday or not. I wish you'd make up your mind and put her out of her misery.'

'Shut up about the bloody balloon.'

'She's got her knickers in a real twist about it.'

'That's her problem.'

Maddy said no more. She got her nail file out and worked on a torn nail. Alan gazed blankly out of the window at the sunny lush fields.

'Let's go for a swim,' he said suddenly. 'Let's take Nick's boat out and swim in the estuary.'

To his surprise, Maddy agreed at once. She normally refused to go into the sea until August. 'It'll be freezing, but never mind. I feel so hot and sticky.'

'Let's hope Mum isn't home yet, or she'll chain us to the house.'

'Are you going in that balloon?'

'No.'

'Tell her, then. Take the pressure off her.'

'I'll tell her when I want to. Don't interfere.'

Angie and Luke hadn't returned, so Alan and Maddy bicycled off to Stagwell Quay immediately. They had permission to use the Popes' old dinghy whenever they wanted. They pushed it down to the water's edge, muddy sand squidging behind their toes. Alan rowed off strongly, in the opposite direction from the power station.

'They'll never tell us if the water's contaminated, so let's keep our distance. Not that it will make much difference.'

Maddy, sitting in the stern, turned her head to look at the power station. A large freighter was sailing past it, completely dwarfed. 'It's so massive. I always forget how massive it is.' She sat back again. 'It does seem mean to put it in such a beautiful place.'

'They always put them in beautiful places. Nuclear power stations are greedy things. They need masses of water, so you'll always find them by rivers and sea-coasts, as isolated as possible. Just the sort of places that are bound to be beautiful.'

'Chernobyl wasn't isolated.'

'But the surroundings are — were — beautiful apparently. Nice river, boating, swimming, fishing, woods all round.' The dinghy rocked violently as the wake of the passing freighter reached them. 'Whoops.'

'By the way, I don't mind helping you with SCAND once the exams are over.' Maddy spoke lightly. Alan took care not to show any surprise.

'Great. You could help on Saturday week.' He told her about dropping Nirex pamphlets into the 'nuclear waste' bin. Maddy giggled.

'What else is happening?'

'The blockade is set for Monday morning, and at the same time banners are going to be hung on the nearest motorway bridges ready for the rush hour to London. But the blockade is the big thing. We're all going to be involved in that, night and day. It'll be fun.' Alan took off his T-shirt. 'Not as much fun as going up in the balloon, but what the hell!'

'Who's going up instead of you?'

Alan did not answer; he was busy shipping the oars and dropping the small anchor over the side. 'Let's swim. You go first, go on.'

'No, you. I might change my mind.'

'Coward.' Alan jumped in, gasping as his hot skin hit the water. 'Terrific.' He swam energetically up and down, dived under the boat, lay on his back and stared at the sky. 'Terrific. There's quite a pull from the tide.'

'I can feel it.' Maddy was trailing her hand in the water.

'Come on in.'

'In a minute.' Maddy gazed with pleasure at the expanse of estuary between the long low spits of land which inperceptibly shaded off into open sea. The Saxon chapel, on the only high land, stuck up like a head peering over a wall. Trees full of rooks clustered near it.

'I like this part of the world.'

'Come on, Maddy.'

'It's too cold.'

Alan began splashing her. 'It's not cold once you get used to it.'

'Beast.'

Suddenly Maddy got up and made herself jump in. She screamed loudly at the cold, and thrashed her arms and legs about.

'This is torture.'

'Three times round the boat. Race you. You start.'

The race degenerated into splashing sessions, until

141

both of them trod water peacefully, one hand on the boat. Gulls called and swooped above them.

'I wish I'd done this every day of the exams. I feel a hundred times better.'

Maddy was staring at the Stagwell shoreline.

'It's funny. Today is the very first day I've realised what an eyesore that power station is. I've always totally accepted it up to now. Just like I accept the chapel. I never thought twice. But it's not a bit like the chapel, is it? Not one tiny little bit.' She shivered. 'I'm cold. I want to get back into the boat. Easier said than done.'

Alan eventually pushed her up and in, and then hauled himself in while the dinghy rocked madly. While he was pulling up the anchor, a fishing boat chugged by. The man at the tiller shouted to them: 'Do you want a tow? You'll find it hard rowing against this tide.'

'Yes, please.'

The boat circled round them, and Alan caught the painter thrown at him and secured it round a thwart. He sat back in the stern with Maddy; they trailed their hands in the creamy churning water behind them. Gulls kept level with the fishing boat, sensing a catch of fish.

'How will they get rid of it when it's worn out?' asked Maddy. They both stared at the looming power station.

'They decommission it.'

'What does that actually mean?'

'No one really knows. It hasn't happened here yet. In the States they're decommissioning their first by taking it to bits and floating it down-river to be buried somewhere else. It's costing more to do that than it did to build the bloody thing in the first place.'

'Crazy.'

'Mr Hawkes says that there's no chance our reactors will be removed when they've finished their useful lives. Stagwell Mound is getting old. Soon they'll just seal it up and leave it. It'll be there to ruin the coastline for several thousand years. And, even if they took it apart, what would they do with the radioactive cores? There's nowhere in Britain they would be allowed to bury a reactor core.'

Maddy wrapped her towel closely round herself; she was still shivering. 'It's like all those horrid fairy-stories where nasty little dwarfs give people presents to make their lives easier, and it always goes wrong in the end. Live now, pay later. God, I'm so cold my teeth are chattering.'

The fishing boat cast them off at the quay and went on to its moorings. Alan and Maddy pulled the dinghy up the beach and then quickly changed out of their wet things. Maddy pulled a couple of cereal and honey bars out of a pocket. Alan stood chewing his and gazing blankly at the power station.

'Come on, Alan. I can't bear to look at that thing any longer.'

'It's not nuclear war that's going to ruin the world. It's those damned things. There's too many of them already.'

'I'm off. I've had enough doom for one day.'

Alan did not mention the balloon, and nor did his mother. She was edgy on Sunday morning but, again, neither said anything. Then, towards midday, Angie shouted excitedly from the garden: 'Alan! Alan! Come and look!'

Swinging gently through the air above Stagwell was a red-and-white-striped hot-air balloon. Hanging from it was a long yellow banner of silk with black letters down it: NO NUCLEAR DUMPS. From the bottom

143

of the banner hung streamers like the tails of Chinese kites. The banner had clearly been weighted, because it hung straight and hardly moved off vertical even though the balloon was travelling relatively fast.

The red and white stripes bulged against the blue sky; heads moved in the basket, but were too high up to be easily identified. The banner moved majestically inland past Stagwell, trumpeting its message. Balloon and banner were mesmerising. Alan watched them raptly as they sailed silently on. He thought he saw Kathy's dark head.

'Isn't it a marvellous sight?' Angie was over-enthusiastic in her relief that the balloon was up there and her son was down here.

Alan said nothing, his eyes following the balloon until it went out of sight, screened by trees. Kathy was up there, having a unique experience instead of him. And she was up there with Guy. Both facts made him acutely miserable. He wanted to shout and curse at his mother, and if she'd made any further remarks to him he would have. But luckily she returned to her weeding, and he went back upstairs and flung himself face downwards on his bed. His eyes were full of the balloon's tight curves of red and white, and the long yellow strip against the blue sky.

CHERNOBYL REACTORS TO RESTART IN OCTOBER
Will they never learn?

Daily Chronicle

FOURTEEN
Friday, 20 June

The weather cooled down for the last week of the exams, and this reduced the physical unpleasantness of sitting for hours crouched over a desk, writing. Even so, the sense of relief Alan felt when he made his last full stop on his final paper was the most intense he'd experienced in his life. When it was all over he just sat there, flaccidly gazing at the scratches and graffiti on the desklid. *Sue loves Mick. . . . Don't let the bastards grind you down. . . .*

'Aren't you ever going to move?' Nick's hand prodded his back. Alan shook himself and stood up. The room had emptied without him even hearing it. 'Come on. Let's get the hell out of here.' Alan followed Nick down the stairs and out into the playground. It was half-past twelve and beginning to rain.

'I fancy a bag of chips and a good film. Let's go and see what's on at the Odeon.'

'I've got to get back to Stagwell.' Alan had received a note from Paul Norrington saying a guide would be waiting for him at two o'clock at the entrance of the power station. 'I've got an appointment this afternoon.'

Nick looked disappointed. 'I thought we'd agreed

to do something after the exams. Originally it was fishing—'

'Let's go fishing tomorrow afternoon.'

'There won't be time. Dad says he needs everybody to help get the blockade ready.'

'We'll find time. I'm sorry about today.'

'I think I'll go and see the Clint Eastwood at the ABC. See you.'

Alan got drenched biking home. He knew Nick was hurt, and felt guilty about not inviting him to come to the power station as well. Nick and Maddy would be livid when they found out he'd been just with Kathy. The trouble was that neither of them seemed to like Kathy, and Alan knew he couldn't cope with the three of them together.

The house was empty. He went into the kitchen and made himself a massive fry-up: bacon, sausages, leftovers of potato and cabbage, chunks of cheese and as an afterthought a sliced banana. He sprinkled Worcester sauce over the lot and took the plateful up to his bedroom. He'd always liked eating in bed; he ensconced himself against the corner wall, and propped the paper open at the sports page. For twenty minutes he was totally happy. He briefly contemplated not turning up at the meeting-point he'd given Kathy. He hadn't seen her since the balloon trip, though she'd rung up and excitedly described it all. Kathy's moped was parked at the side of the road. Kathy herself was standing beside a large noticeboard.

STAGWELL MOUND NUCLEAR POWER STATION
PRIVATE ROAD
NO PUBLIC WAY OR VEHICLE ACCESS
BEYOND THIS POINT

The paint was peeling; Kathy was picking at the loose flakes. Behind her against the grey clouds was the greyer bulk of the power station. The whine was loud.

'Won't they stop us as we ride down there?'

'Paul said he'd given our names to the man at the gates.'

Kathy's eyes were shining with anticipation inside her helmet. 'Come on, then, let's go.' She drove her moped slowly so that Alan could keep pace with her.

'You're not planning anything, are you?' he shouted.

'What? Can't hear.'

'You're not going to make your own one-man demo, for instance?'

'What, me? As if I would.' Kathy revved her bike without looking at him.

'Don't do anything crazy, Kathy.'

'Don't nag, Alan.' She looked annoyed. 'Relax. I'm just seeing over the place, that's all.'

They left their bikes in the car park and walked up to the clerk in the gatehouse, who eyed them suspiciously.

'Mr Norrington has arranged for us to see round.'

With an expression which implied that he thought this unlikely, the clerk picked up a list. 'Alan Page, Madeleine Page, Kathy Wilson. There's only two of you.'

'My sister couldn't come.'

'I'll just check with Mr Norrington.' After telephoning he turned and even smiled at them. 'He's coming along himself. Put these badges on, please, and return them when you leave.'

Alan and Kathy stared at the two reactors as they waited. The whine didn't seem any louder close up. There were lawns all round, and beds full of neat rows of red and yellow flowers. Paul Norrington came out of a nearby office talking to another man.

'Hullo, Alan. How do you do, Kathy? I've asked Gerry Steadman here to show you round. I'm sorry I can't do it myself but I've got a heavy schedule this afternoon. Pleased to see you both, anyway. A pity Maddy couldn't come as well.' Paul bustled off, and Gerry Steadman took them to a reception centre where there was a lecture-hall and working model of the station.

'Now, let's have a quick decko at the model, though I suggest you come back and look at it again when you've seen over the whole place. It'll make more sense.'

The model was ten feet high and fifteen or so wide, and showed a cross-section of the working parts of the whole station — reactor, boiler, circulator, turbo-alternator, and finally transformer. The simulated spherical reactor glowed red as the mechanism raised the control rods; the lurid red light faded as the rods were lowered.

'I didn't know the reactor was round,' said Alan.

'That's actually the pressure vessel containing the reactor core.' Gerry Steadman smacked his hand against the model, which wobbled a bit.

'It looks like a spaceship.' Kathy prodded various parts.

'Right, let's go on to the real thing. I thought we'd begin by going straight to the charge floor; that's this flat part here directly above the reactor core. Okey-dokey?'

'Fine,' said Alan.

'Take a helmet.'

He gave them each standard bright-yellow helmets; Kathy got the giggles when Alan put his on.

'You look like Donald Duck.'

'Belt up.' Alan stalked ahead, close to Gerry Steadman.

'You're lucky to see the place on your own. People usually go round in groups. Relatives of Mr Norrington's, are you?'

'No, just friends.'

'I like to see youngsters getting VIP treatment.'

Kathy's hat fell off with a clatter as a gust of wind came round the side of the reactor building. 'Oops.' She giggled again. Alan started feeling annoyed with her. He couldn't think why she was being so silly. Gerry Steadman took her hat and patiently tightened the strap, and then led them into the reactor. He took them through a turnstile which he unlocked with a special key, and then led them up a staircase painted in bright cheerful colours ('Window-dressing,' muttered Kathy). They went through a lobby where a group of businessmen were checking their hands and clothing for radiation. Gerry Steadman led Alan and Kathy into the reactor hall itself.

'You're now on the charge floor. Below you are about 2,600 fuel channels filled with fuel rods.'

'I feel as if my feet ought to be tingling,' said Alan. 'How big's the actual core?'

'It's a vertical cylinder of about forty-five feet in diameter, thirty feet high, built up of graphite blocks. These contain the fuel channels. Then this core is contained in a spherical steel pressure vessel which in turn is surrounded by a concrete biological shield at least eight feet thick.'

'Even with all that, isn't this the most dangerous place in the power station?' asked Kathy.

Gerry Steadman smiled at her, the smile of one who's heard that same comment many times before. 'Not dangerous. We don't use the word *dangerous*. It's inaccurate. This charge floor is absolutely safe. Even when the charge machine is removing highly radioactive spent fuel rods, the whole operation is carried out in such a way and with so many safety precautions that there's no danger to the operators.' He pointed to a huge crane-like machine spanning the hall. 'That's the charge machine; it moves up and down on its rails.'

'At Chernobyl, the blast knocked their charge machine right over.' Alan gazed at the vast solid-looking structure. He looked above him. 'And the top of the hall was blown open, wasn't it?'

'How does this compare with Chernobyl for size?' asked Kathy.

'Chernobyl is four times bigger. This is a 250 megawatt reactor, and the one that blew up was a 1000. But rest assured, an explosion like the Russian one couldn't happen here.'

'Why not?'

'Our reactors are programmed to shut down if there's any hint of trouble.'

'So were theirs.'

Gerry Steadman didn't pick up Kathy's comment because at that moment a man hurried by saying something to Gerry as he passed and pointing behind him.

'You're in luck. Would you like to see some fuel rods close up?'

'But aren't fuel rods the most radioactive things in the whole place . . .?' began Alan nervously.

Gerry laughed. 'They are, when they're either in the core or spent. But not when they're fresh. Follow me.'

In a small room off the Reactor Hall, a crowd of men were unpacking and laying out shiny cylinders, cylinders which looked like long thin silver cigars, or rockets. Men in protective clothing were handling them, but two other men were bent over close, inspecting the rods.

'Pretty, aren't they? Uranium rods about an inch in diameter, sheathed in magnesium alloy. They're safe to touch, but your hands would contaminate them — you'd damage the surface. Those men are wearing gloves to protect the rods, not their hands.'

Some of the rods were being carefully stacked into a square metal container.

'That container will be put in the charge machine very soon, and those new rods will be lowered into the core.'

Alan bent over to look closely at the shiny cylinders, so innocent now, so lethal soon. 'How long is the life of a fuel rod?'

'Three to eight years, depending on where they are in the core. Those in the centre wear out quickest.'

'Then what happens to them?' Kathy hovered behind everyone, looking uneasy.

'When they've been withdrawn, they're sealed in special flasks and left to cool in the ponds.'

'Ponds!' Alan had a vision of the pond behind Nick's farm, scummy with algae and leaves, well trodden and messed up round the edges by the ducks and geese.

'There are cooling-ponds adjacent to each reactor, below ground-level. The flasks are slipped mechanically in and stay there for at least nine months.'

'Then the baby is born and it's transported to Sellafield to be reprocessed and cause more radio-active waste.' Kathy's voice was followed by a silence.

'You could put it like that,' said Gerry. His smile didn't reach his eyes this time. 'Time to move on.' As he led them back into the reactor hall, Kathy asked where the ponds actually were.

'Just through there. From certain places, you can see the spent rods glowing as they cool down. Now, before we go on to the turbine hall, we must use the

151

monitor to check our radiation levels. Hands first, then clothes and shoes.' To Gerry's surprise, the sole of Kathy's right shoe was contaminated. She looked horrified as the dial registered this.

'My God.'

'No cause for worry. This happens occasionally. You could have stepped on a drop of contaminated oil. But it's a very low level of contamination, and it'll wash off. Watch.' He took the shoe to a row of basins, and ran water over the sole for a few minutes. Then he put the geiger counter against the shoe again, and the reading was normal. 'There you are. Clean again.'

'But have I been radiated?'

'Of course not. That's a minute patch of contamination. It'll have no effect on you at all.'

Kathy gingerly slipped her shoe on again, looking unconvinced. 'I wasn't aware I'd stepped on anything unusual. So it is dangerous in there. This proves it. I think I'll throw these shoes away when I get home.' But Alan could see Kathy was excited by what had happened. Her eyes had their familiar gleam under that silly yellow hat.

Gerry took them out through another scanner and then along a high enclosed walkway which linked the reactor building with the turbine hall and the control room.

'Can't we go straight to the control room?' asked Kathy.

'There's a group of businessmen in there at the moment. It's better to wait till they've finished; the control room's not very big. Have a mint?'

They stopped while Gerry handed round a tattered bag of glacier mints. Rain beat against the glass walls of the walkway, which looked out on to the sea on one side and fields on the other. Alan pointed.

'Isn't that Saxon's Field, the proposed nuclear-waste dump-site?'

'Yes — over to the left, beyond those sheds.'

'What do you think about it?' Alan gave Kathy a warning dig when she seemed on the point of interrupting.

'A lot of fuss about nothing. A well-managed nuclear-waste dump couldn't harm anybody.' Gerry started to walk on, dismissing the whole business.

'But don't you think it's wrong to litter the country-side with waste-dumps, in case things go wrong?' Alan kept his voice even; Kathy said nothing, having got the message. 'Shouldn't the Government develop really deep shafts, under the seabed if possible?'

' 'Course they should, in the long run.' Gerry stopped walking and offered his mints round again. 'No? I eat tons of sweets to take my mind off the non-smoking rule in this place. Yes, under the sea would be an answer, but it would be astronomically expensive. By the way, Nirex is nothing to do with us, you know. Between you and me I think they've handled the locals very badly. I'm a local myself. I live on the main road to Maldham. Someone came and asked me to sign the petition against the dump, and I told them they were fighting the wrong issue. They should be worried about all the extra traffic — lots of lorries from other power stations — and not about the piffling radiation risk. If they'd asked me to sign on the traffic issue, I would have.' He marched on. Kathy whispered: 'Why aren't we arguing with him?'

'What's the point? He's bound to clam up. Keep your cool, Kathy.'

Kathy got bored in the big noisy turbine hall; Alan and Gerry went on and on about condensers and generators and transformers and switch-gear. She went over to an old man on duty who said his name was Sid. He was having his tea break.

'I've worked here since the reactor became critical in August 1961. Twenty-five years—'

'Critical?'

'Ah, that's a term used to describe a reactor when the nuclear power is balanced. Not increasing, not decreasing. You ask them about that in the control room. Well, I happened to start work here on the day the reactor first became critical. Like you, I was puzzled by that word when I first heard it.'

'Don't let me stop you eating your tea.'

'You won't, girl.' He took another sandwich, offering her one as well.

'No, thanks all the same. But tell me, doesn't it worry you that you've worked in a nuclear environment for twenty-five whole years?'

Sid rolled his eyes while he finished chewing a mouthful. 'All you folks outside seem to think this place has radioactivity leaking out like steam in a laundry. It's safe in here. It's safe everywhere. I can see you don't believe me. Bet you're a member of Greenpeace.'

'Well, I am in fact—'

'Don't tell Gerry over there; he starts foaming at the mouth if he hears the word Greenpeace.' Sid disposed of his sandwich in a last huge mouthful. 'I've got nothing against Greenpeace, mind; they do a lot of good around the world. But they don't listen — they always know best. And they never believe a word we say, ever. It gets guides like Gerry down, because of all the argument and mistrust.' Sid belched gently. 'Pardon me. Cucumber always makes me do that. The wife keeps saying I ought to give cucumber up, but I like it.'

Gerry and Alan were starting to leave, so she

thanked Sid for talking to her and caught them up.

'That old chap's been here twenty-five years.'

'Really? I'm enjoying this, aren't you? It's much more interesting than I expected.'

'You'll be getting a job here next.'

'Don't be silly.'

'You're swallowing everything he tells you.'

'I am not. But it's important to hear the other side.'

Kathy grunted. Gerry was waiting for them at a security checkpoint. They followed him through to the control room.

It was like being inside an egg yolk. The entire wall area, full of dials and switches, was faced in yellow; so were the two central control-desks. The room was lit from above; daylight filtered through an orange glass grid.

'The left-hand side controls reactor one and the right hand reactor two. Are you free at the moment, John?' Gerry took them over to the man sitting at the right-hand control-desk. He, too, was having his tea break; he held a large piece of chocolate cake in his hand. Disposable cups of tea steamed here and there. In the middle of the central console, also yellow, was a battered old tin tray on which stood teabags, instant coffee, a bag of sugar and an enormous old-fashioned aluminium hob-kettle. Kathy nudged Alan, pointing to the kettle.

'Do you think they boil it on the hot pipes coming out of the reactor?'

'Shh.'

'Sorry to interrupt your tea break, John.'

'No problem.' John had rolls of fat bulging over his trousers. He licked his fingers while nodding towards a group of smartly suited men who were being shown dials and switches. 'The last lot are still here. Piccadilly Circus today.'

155

'Alan and Kathy would like to know how this works.'

'No problem.' John said this constantly. He explained how, when the reactor was critical, the red line drawn on a graphed gauge remained fairly even, with small fluctuations from side to side. But as the control rods were pulled up or down, the line would start zigzagging to left or right. He turned a well-worn handle labelled *Rod Speed* to the left slightly. There were three indicators: *Up Slow*, *Up Fast*, *Up Very Fast*. John stopped the handle on *Up Slow*, but the effect on the red line was immediate. It bit sharply to the left.

'Tweaking the tail of the dragon,' said Gerry.

John turned the handle back to its former position, and the red line returned to its mean.

'What would happen if the fuel rods got stuck when they were pulled out? How would you shut the reactor off then?' asked Kathy.

'We couldn't, but the situation would never get that far. Long before such a thing could happen, we would have been alerted that faults existed say in the standpipes, and the reactor would have been shut down.'

'Say a mad terrorist came rushing in here and pulled that handle to *Up Fast*? Would there be a surge of heat like in Chernobyl?'

'There's a failsafe trip mechanism which automatically shuts the reactor down. You could go mad with all those handles and nothing would happen.'

'And you've seen the security in this place,' said Gerry.

'But I might be the mad terrorist myself,' said Kathy. She was smiling wickedly. She suddenly plunged her hand into her shoulder-bag, and threw something that hit the main control console with a sharp cracking sound. An appalling smell filled the control room within seconds. The businessmen started calling out in alarm. John swore and rushed forward to the console. Kathy began to shout: 'Radiation stinks! Radiation stinks!' again and again.

Gerry, white-faced with anger, was reassuring everybody. 'It's only a stink bomb. That stupid girl's thrown it. Relax everyone. It's a kid's stink bomb.'

'Radiation stinks! Radiation stinks!'

Alan stood frozen throughout all this. He was furious with Kathy for this ridiculous act of protest. He wanted to disappear through the floor with embarrassment.

'Out. Get out.' Gerry took Kathy by the arm. The smell was still appalling. John was mopping at a patch of chemical and almost retching.

'Radiation stinks! It's a pity we can't smell or see it!' Kathy's voice filled the control room as she was led out. Some of the businessmen were talking together as they followed. Alan heard one say: 'Amazing girl. The trouble is she has a point.'

'There are better ways of making it,' snapped Gerry.

'But you have to admit it was colourful.'

Alan could see Kathy grinning away outside the control room, dead pleased with herself. She was joined by the sympathetic businessman as Gerry shepherded everyone out. Alan kept his distance from her, and tried to get near Gerry to apologise.

'I'm sorry my friend did that.'

Gerry looked at him with suspicion. 'Bloody silly thing to do. Why didn't you stop her?'

'She didn't let me in on it.' Because she knew I'd have said don't do it, thought Alan bitterly. She's achieved nothing at all, just put a lot of backs up.

Stink bombs. He looked angrily at Kathy's animated back view as she chattered to her new acquaintance.

Very frostily, Gerry personally saw Alan and Kathy out of the main gates. As they walked to the car park, Kathy said: 'That man I talked to knows a journalist on the *Daily Mail*. He's going to make sure something goes in about my little stink.'

'Bully for you.'

'Tut, tut. We are in a disapproving mood. Guy thought it was a great idea.'

'Leave Guy out of this, will you? You lied to me, Kathy.'

'Lied?'

'You said you weren't going to do anything.'

'I didn't actually lie. I let you believe what you wanted to believe.'

'Sounds like lying to me.'

Kathy stared at him, cold with anger. 'Look, Alan, there are times when the end justifies the means. I thought it was important to make that protest, and I was pretty sure you'd try to stop me because of this friend of your mother's working at the station. So I played it my way.'

'You mean, you made use of me to get into the place, and then lied to me.'

'Look at it any way you like. I know which way I think is right.'

They glared at each other before unlocking their bikes in silence. Kathy started her engine and with a mocking 'Thanks for fixing the visit' rode away with a spurt of gravel. Alan bicycled slowly home in the rain.

CHERNOBYL, RURAL RESORT

It was a land of lakes, sandy soils, forests and water meadows. There was fishing in the river and bathing in the many small lakes. The nearby woods were always full of berries and wild mushrooms.

There were over 100 farms and villages within 30 km of the power station. Almost 100,000 people lived and worked in the area. They grew flax, potatoes, maize, rapeseed, soya and beet. The nearest farm was only 14 km away from the nuclear plant; it had over 4,000 workers, 6,500 head of cattle, 1,500 pigs and sheep. The workers are gone; the animals are dead.

From *The Worst Accident in the World*

FIFTEEN
Saturday, 21 June;
Sunday, 22 June

Stagwell High Street was full of shoppers on a fine Saturday morning when Ken eased his truck along to a corner near the Nirex information shop. He and Nick lowered the large, neatly repainted yellow bin with NUCLEAR WASTE written on all four sides and placed it in the middle of the wide pavement. Immediately Alan, followed at a short distance by Maddy, entered the shop.

All Stagwell children had loved the old sweetshop, crammed with big bottles holding humbugs, toffees, fruit drops of every shape and colour and flavour — more kinds of boiled sweet than one could believe existed. The old lady who had owned it had always waited patiently while her clients stood in agonies of indecision over what to spend their pocket-money on.

To see it stripped down to a few smart display units filled only with pamphlets was painful to Alan, though he noticed it still smelt faintly of sweets — of caramel and chocolate and sugar. Alan smiled at the young man behind a desk and helped himself to a complete range of pamphlets. They were called Fact Sheets, with titles like *What is Radioactivity?*, *What Is Nirex?*, *What is a Radioactive Waste Repository?*, *How do Geological Barriers Work?* Alan opened one which was subtitled *How Long Can Concrete Last?* and saw it was full of glossy photos, including one with the caption: *A 1,700-year-old sample of Roman concrete recovered during restoration work on Hadrian's wall.*

As he was walking along skimming through this pamphlet, Robin Hawkes tapped him on the shoulder. 'I shouldn't bother to read it; it's a load of the usual windy optimism.' Hawkes took the pamphlet and laughed. 'I love this sentence. *If concrete is such a durable material, then why do we have a problem with concrete structures?* Why, indeed. But Nirex are going to solve these problems of course — *by good design, selection of appropriate materials and good workmanship*. No one in the nuclear industry ever seems to take into account the destructive effect on standards of the average workman, British or otherwise.'

'Typical they chose the colour green.' Alan held up the bunch of pamphlets; all were a spring-like green. 'It's like the nuclear ads on telly. They always show acres of rolling unspoilt countryside and play English folksongs arranged for string orchestra as background music.'

Hawkes laughed again. 'The horrible square pile of a power station away in the far distance becomes lost in all the pastoral romanticism.'

'They hope.'

'It works, unfortunately. People are easily influenced by mood, music and colour.' He flung his handful of pamphlets into the yellow dustbin. So did Alan.

There was a steady stream of supporters going in and out of the Nirex shop. More and more publicity material dropped into the bin; it was filling up nicely. A reporter appeared, then another. A television crew followed. Word was quickly getting about that a visual joke was being played out in the High Street; crowds of people started to collect.

Mark Ableman came flapping down the street in his long black cassock. 'I hope I'm not too late. Been doing a funeral.'

'They're trying to shut the shop. Some of my pupils have just been turned out; they weren't allowed to take any stuff at all.' Hawkes looked very cheerful. 'Have a bash, Mark.'

Mark Ableman sailed into the little shop. The young man in charge was on the phone, clearly trying to get advice. When he saw the vicar's dog collar and cassock, he waved him over to the depleted stacks of pamphlets on the shelves.

'If you don't mind, I'll take a handful of everything. All very interesting, I must say.'

The young man put his hand over the mouthpiece. 'Fine, go ahead.' Mark Ableman did not empty the shelves, but he took enough to make a serious dent in the remainder. He then handed them all out to the disappointed crowd of children who'd been hanging about outside.

'Thanks. Great.'

'Now let us process to the wastebin.' And showers more leaflets dropped in.

'I feel sorry for that young man,' said the vicar to Robin Hawkes. 'He's getting very upset, and it's not his fault. He's just doing a job.'

A fat lady with a basket full of groceries was the next person to try to enter. She was obviously a genuine enquirer, but the young man refused to give her anything. He firmly locked the shop from the inside and disappeared. The lady was furious.

'Bloody cheek. They open an information centre and won't give you their stuff. Bloody cheek I call it.' Then she saw the NUCLEAR WASTE signs on the bin, and all the pamphlets inside it. She grew even angrier.

'It's people like you that give a bad name to Stagwell. You're not representing all of us, you know. Not by any means.' She glared at Ken. 'I happen to want to read those.'

'Help yourself, Mrs Ramsbotham.' He picked up a bundle of pamphlets and let them run through his fingers. 'You won't learn much you didn't know already. It's all waffle.'

'I don't need you to tell me what to think, Ken Pope.' She rootled in the bin, taking out different titles, seemingly unaware of the camera filming the scene.

'Make sure you've got one of each, Mrs Ramsbotham. They're all free. Look, you haven't got *Why Do We Need to Do Research?* That's very weighty, very weighty indeed.' Ken was enjoying himself.

Nick hid in a shop doorway, hands over his eyes.

'And don't miss this one. It's a really good read. *Radioactive Waste: What Are the Options?*' Ken's voice boomed out dramatically. 'You'll be relieved to know that radioactivity is much better than

162

chemical wastes like mercury, arsenic and asbestos, because — listen to this, Mrs Ramsbotham — 'the potential hazard of radioactive waste reduces with time.' Well, what are we all worrying about? Caesium 137 and Strontium 90 have a half-life of only thirty years; Carbon 14's a bit of a looney of course with a half-life of over five thousand years, but don't let's worry about that. . . .'

Mrs Ramsbotham had a haunted look on her face by this time. She grabbed at the leaflet in Ken's hand and pushed her way through the large and appreciative crowd. At that point a traffic warden came up and asked Ken to move his truck.

'Look, I'm making a political protest.'

'You're causing an obstruction. I got no choice, mate. Either you move or I book you.'

'Come on, Ken.' Hawkes took Ken's arm. The crowd started to drift away. The reporters had already gone. 'We've made our point. Let's go. We don't want them to reclaim their leaflets.'

They loaded the full bin into the back of the truck, but Ken had no intention of taking it home. He, Nick and Alan drove to Maldham instead, and put the wastebin on a stone plinth in front of the Town Hall in the main square. Well pleased, they drove back to the farm to put the finishing touches to St George and the dragon.

Sophy Robertson had become a firm friend of Ken's over the construction of these two. St George was built on a skeleton of chicken wire; Sophy had borrowed some plastic armour from a theatre. He was splendid, but the dragon was a triumph. They had used a forage harvester, with its pointed reptilian-like head. Sophy had cleverly covered the cardboard scales with words. From a distance they looked like rough scales, but close up one could read: *meltdown, fallout, gamma rays, beta rays, alpha rays*. . . . The dragon's wide mouth and long tongue were covered with the word *radiation* written in red. He was altogether a fearsome warning with comic undertones; when Ken towed him up next day from the Quay to Tanner's Corner, he attracted a lot of delighted laughter from all who passed him. Ken and Sophy planned to have St George on one side of the road, and the dragon on the other, moving them together when the road was to be blocked.

'They're mostly for the kids, of course,' said Ken, staring fondly at his handiwork, now safely installed behind Ollie Tanner's garage on the main road.

'Speak for yourself,' said Sophy, patting the dragon. 'We must stop the telly cameras filming them until they're in position.'

'Liked your banner, Mrs Robertson,' said Ollie Tanner, who was looking slightly dazed as the SCAND committee unloaded all the equipment for the blockade.

'I was pleased with it, too. Glad I remembered to weight it down properly. Well, Ken, I'm off. See you here on Monday morning. I'll have to bring my children until it's time for school.'

'They'll be coming anyway if they're at St George's Primary. The whole school is turning out.'

Alan was sitting on a pile of sandbags talking to Nick when he heard the familiar sound of a moped. For the first time, his heart didn't beat any faster when he saw it was Kathy. Friday was still heavy inside him.

'Here comes trouble,' muttered Nick. Alan for once agreed with him. Kathy came right up to them before she switched off her engine. She stayed astride her bike.

'My little demonstration got into the Sunday papers,' she said. ' "Radiation stinks" is now a national catchword. For a day or two.'

'What demonstration?' asked Nick.

'Hasn't Alan told you about our visit to the power station?'

'No.' Alan groaned inwardly as Kathy gave a brief summary of the visit. There was a pause when she'd finished.

'Thanks a ton for inviting me.' Nick stood up, looking angry and refusing to meet Alan's eyes. 'You're a good friend, I must say.' He walked off.

'My, my,' said Kathy. 'We *are* touchy today.'

'Shut up.' Alan wanted to follow Nick, who had disappeared behind Ollie's garage. 'I should have asked him.'

'Why didn't you, then?'

'Because he can't stand you, that's why. I couldn't handle the two of you together, that's why.'

Alan saw the pain in Kathy's green eyes before she turned her face away. 'Oh dear. I had no idea I was so unpopular,' she said lightly. Her foot suddenly kicked the moped into life again. 'I'll take myself off, in that case. See you.'

Alan opened his mouth, but could not find the right words. Kathy rode off, making a very tight turn as she did so. She was watched by several people; she was an expert rider, there was no doubt about that. Her yellow shirt ballooned out over her black leggings. Then she was gone.

'Who's that?' Ollie Tanner stared after her. He was a small wizened man with a lecherous reputation. Alan shrugged.

'A girl from my school.'

'Saucy piece, eh?'

Alan ignored Ollie and went round the back of

the garage to find Nick. He had gone into Ollie's little back room, which contained a gas-ring and an electric kettle, a couple of dented dirty pans and some equally dirty chipped crockery, all surrounded by oily nuts and bolts and bits of engine. There was a pair of wooden chairs, also smeared all over with oil. On the walls were pages of a pin up calendar; naked girls draped over the bonnets of cars. The little room stank of cigarette smoke. Since Ollie was not allowed to smoke on the forecourt, he shut himself in here.

'Ugh. What a fug.' Alan stubbed out a dog-end left burning in a cracked saucer. Nick was leafing through Ollie's Sunday paper. He did not look up.

'Nick, I'm really sorry you didn't come with us. I didn't ask you because of Kathy — I know you don't like her.'

'Don't mind her either way. She doesn't bother me.'

'I thought she did.'

Nick didn't answer. Alan fiddled with a spanner. Finally Nick burst out: 'You bloody well knew how much I wanted to see inside the station. We've often discussed it. That's why I was annoyed. I felt let down. Kathy comes along and in five minutes you're inside the place.'

This time Alan didn't answer. Then Ollie came in and put the kettle on. 'Where's me fag? I left one burning.'

'Must've gone out.'

Ollie glared at the boys. 'One of you finished it, I suppose.'

'We don't smoke, Ollie.'

Ollie sniffed at the stub on the saucer. 'I always burn 'em down more than that.'

'Ruin your lungs.'

'When I want advice from you boys, I'll ask.'

A crowd of women led by Pam Webb suddenly appeared outside. 'Ollie, we've come to set up camp. If we could run a power cable from somewhere to the tent, that would be marvellous. We don't want to swamp your facilities' — Pam looked into the oily little dump — 'so we're setting up a refreshment tent on the verge over there, if you're agreeable.'

'Fine, fine. Let me come and have a look.' Ollie bustled out.

'I distinctly saw cash-till signs in his eyes,' muttered Alan. 'This blockade is going to mean good business for Mr Tanner.'

Nick passed over the Sunday paper in silence, pointing to a small piece.

STINK BOMBS IN POWER STATION

'Radiation stinks,' says pretty Kathy Wilson, aged 17, 'so I thought I'd draw attention to the fact.'

'I was really angry when she did that.' Alan tossed the paper aside. 'I thought it was childish. I didn't want to know.'

'That girl likes publicity.'

'You can say that again.'

'Boys.' Pam stuck her head through the door. 'The scaffolding towers have arrived and need unloading. Come along now, we need you.'

'Boss, boss, boss,' said Nick when she'd gone. 'She's going to drive me mad. She thinks she's Napoleon.'

Alan laughed. 'We'd better go, before your dad does his back in again.'

'Hang on a minute.' Nick hesitated. 'Look, I'm sorry I got so annoyed. I was jealous, that's all. I can easily fix myself a visit round the station some time.'

'They're keen on visitors now. Things have changed since Chernobyl. Take Maddy, too — I know she wants to go. She'll be just as mad as you when she learns I've been without her.'

'Boys!'

'Coming.'

'So's Christmas.'

'Old bat.'

HUGE NEW REACTOR SITED NEAR CITY
As a gesture of faith in nuclear power, the Russians
have announced that a giant reactor of the Chernobyl
design but 50 per cent greater in capacity, will begin
operating later this year. . . .

The Guardian

SIXTEEN
Monday, 23 June

Alan woke at dawn and lay listening to the birds. He
was alert at once. It was pointless lying in bed. He
got up and crept downstairs to get a glass of orange
juice. The fridge was almost empty, and there was
no orange juice. No eggs, no bacon. Monday. It was
always the same on Monday; everything ran out.
Angie did a big shop on her way back from school,
but breakfast on Mondays could be a strange meal.

Alan looked in the storecupboard. Baked beans,
sweetcorn. A tin of ham that had been there so long
it was probably poisonous. Mandarin segments. He
took the beans out, opened the tin and spooned some
on to a piece of crispbread. As he ate he went to the
kitchen door and unlocked it. The sky outside was
a radiant peachy colour; everything in the garden
glowed, fresh and damply scented. A spider had made
his web across the door during the night; its filaments
shone against the dawning sunlight, while the spider
was still busy extending his web. Alan watched the
spider for a while, wondering what possessed it to

169

build its web just there, where it would inevitably be swept away by Angie or Maddy, neither of whom could abide spiders. Alan liked them. He had always been able to pick up any sort of crawling thing.

It'll be magical down on the estuary. As soon as this thought entered his mind he decided to go down there. He spooned out some more baked beans. He felt intensely happy. It was the first Monday morning for ages when he didn't have a horrible exam, or the work for a horrible exam, looming in front of him. He felt as light as the spider, and wished he could spin his happiness into an equally beautiful web.

He bicycled down the longer route, past the Saxon chapel. Rows of gulls were standing on its gabled roof. He went round the chapel on his bike, and the gulls rose noisily into the air and started circling towards the estuary, calling in alarm. Alan bumped towards the hide, and then stood looking out over the marsh at the distant North Sea. He saw a lone birdwatcher already out there, making for the hide where he had seen his mother with Paul.

He still didn't know what had really happened between Angie and Paul but, whatever it was, it seemed to be over. These days Angie spent all her spare time typing furiously to earn extra money for the summer holiday.

He watched the sun above the marsh; its deep orange disc had wisps of cloud across it. Birds swooped and dipped, black against the sun. There was a golden sword of light on the sea, its point towards the sun. As the sun rose, the sword widened to a wedge-shaped carpet of gold.

Yet through it all Alan was aware of the ever-present whine. He turned his bike suddenly, and shouted aloud towards the power station: *'Shut up!'* Why should the buggers risk us losing our world, all for a bit of extra electricity? Why? As Alan free-wheeled down the hill towards Stagwell Quay, it seemed quite mad. All the calm reasoned arguments of the technicians in the power station faded into nonsense before the beauty of the sunrise, the light on the sea, the calling swooping seabirds.

The Nirex convoy was due at nine o'clock. By eight o'clock the road beside Ollie Tanner's garage was chaos. Protesters' cars were parked for a mile on both sides of the verge; farmers had come with tractors; schoolchildren were rushing about. They hadn't bothered to go to St George's Primary first because their parents were involved in the demonstration.

On each side of the road was a scaffolding tower, with a banner across proclaiming that Stagwell did not want a nuclear dump. Beside the right-hand tower was St George and on the other side was the dragon. Workers going to the power station passed through and stared in amazed fascination as they went under the arch. A few policemen stood lamely about, talking into their radios, clearly taken aback by the scale of the demonstration.

Alan and Nick were surprised, too. They had somehow expected a hundred or a couple of hundred people at most; in fact by nine o'clock there must have been a thousand or more. A half-mile section of the road was full of people.

The whole of the school had by now arrived in the road. They held placards ranging from polite ones made under supervision in class — *The children say No to Nirex* — to more blunt ones scrawled at home: *Nuke makes you Puke*. St George's Primary had done an elaborate banner saying *St George's says No to the Nuclear Dragon* which hung from the scaffolding tower. Television cameras and reporters were everywhere. Alan and Nick kept out of sight in Ollie's back room. Ollie himself was near despair.

'I'm not going to get a customer for petrol all day. No one can get by.' He rolled a thin greasy fag. 'I thought all this was going to be good for business.'

'Don't worry, Ollie, you'll get the business. There'll be some sort of action here for days, weeks maybe.'

'What about me tanker delivery?' Ollie stared at Alan morosely. 'They'll never get through. They're due here dinner-time.'

'You won't need a delivery if you don't sell any petrol,' said Nick. 'What you should do is stock up on your sweets and crisps and stuff. You'll do a roaring trade in them all day.'

'But them bloody women are running a buffy out there.'

'Comfort yourself with this, then, Ollie: we're all going to be the losers if Nirex starts dumping here. The sacrifice is worth it.'

'Sacrifices are never worth it,' said Ollie, his fag bouncing on his lip. 'I've tried them and I know.'

There was a roar of excitement from outside, and shouts of 'They're coming! They're coming!'

Alan and Nick rushed out and climbed on to an oil-drum which gave them a good vantage-point over the crowd. But in fact the one vehicle approaching was a large police-van with its light flashing. It edged through the crowd and disgorged a dozen policemen. Alan and Nick went back to Ollie's snuggery, where he was squeezing the last bit of tannin out of a teabag.

'False alarm.'

'What time are they due?' Ollie put powdered milk into his orange brew and added three spoons of sugar. His cigarette dangled, out. Flakes of ash fell in his tea. For a moment Alan thought he might drink his tea with his fag in place. Instead he stuck it behind his ear before sipping appreciatively at his cup.

'Ten minutes ago.'

'They've probably changed the day to fool you all.'

Half an hour went by and other people began to voice the same thought. Children started queuing at the petrol-station lavatory. The buffet was doing a brisk business in tea and coffee. Some of the dragon's scales fell off when two boys had a fight beside it.

Suddenly a murmur spread through the crowd. The convoy had been sighted.

'Fill the road!' shouted Ken. 'Push the thingummy-bobs together!' He gestured wildly at the dragon while he pushed St George. St George's lance promptly fell out and had to be jammed back. But by the time the first vehicle in the convoy of three — car, land-rover and lorry — reached the blockade the gap was closed. Beyond them, the road was full of people chanting and waving their placards.

A smartly dressed man got out of the leading car and looked round for a spokesman. Pam Webb and Robin Hawkes stepped forward.

'I'm Henry Gordon, a director of the consulting engineers appointed by Nirex to conduct this test drilling.' He shook hands energetically with both of them.

A strange silence had fallen all round him, broken only by the sound of the engines of the convoy vehicles idling while they waited. Even the children were quiet. Everyone waited. Then Ken Pope broke the silence.

'You'll not get by us,' he shouted. 'Not today, not tomorrow, not ever. This blockade stays up till you give up.'

'You must remember this is only a test drilling,' began Henry Gordon, but his voice was drowned out. Children shouted, adults shouted, everybody shouted. Soon the shouts became a chant: 'No no no to the nuclear dump! No no no to the nuclear dump!'

The men in the lorry stayed put; the others conferred round the driver of the land-rover. Then the lorry was instructed to reverse away down the narrow country road. Henry Gordon returned to talk to Pam and Robin amid cheers from the crowd when they saw the lorry retreat.

'We'll be back for another try this afternoon. We hope you'll reconsider this blockade. After all, we are simply contractors; we're not a government body. And we're not actually building anything.'

Shouts of 'Go away', 'Thin end of the wedge', 'Get lost' followed Gordon back to his car. He looked annoyed as he reversed away.

Robin Hawkes raised his loud-hailer. 'We've made our first point. All those who can stay, please do. We'll expect the rest of you back at two o'clock. Leave your placard behind the garage, and see you later.'

People dispersed with a slight sense of anticlimax. Ollie came out of his den looking delighted as traffic began to trickle through again. Most of it was connected with the media. The police-van drove off, having maintained a low profile throughout.

Kathy drove up in a flurry, and parked her moped near Alan. 'I couldn't come before. Had a class first thing. What happened?'

'Not a lot.'

'I saw the convoy parked in a layby on the Maldham road.'

As Alan was describing the morning's events to her, Pam came up. 'Would you two like to go down to St George's School and make sure they know they're expected this afternoon? I know the head's prepared to send them again, but we want the children to sit down in organised rows on the road itself, so they need a bit of warning or it'll be bedlam.'

'Come, too,' said Alan to Nick.

'I can't. Dad's asked me to help him mend the dragon.'

'More symbolic if it fell to bits.' Kathy smiled at Nick; she was obviously making an effort.

'Tell Dad that.' He grinned back at her.

So Alan and Kathy went the half-mile on their bikes, Kathy keeping her speed down so that Alan could ride abreast. It was only when they got to the gates of the school that Alan realised his mother would now meet Kathy. He watched Kathy lock up her moped, and take off her helmet. It was a warm day; she was wearing that skimpy T-shirt that revealed her whole shape; her black leggings were on as usual. She seemed to live in them. She looked dead sexy. Alan didn't want Angie to meet her.

'Well, come on.' Kathy swung her helmet backwards and forwards. 'I can see they're all in that hall there.' She pointed to the large glass windows of the hall cum gymnasium. Next to it was Angie's office. Alan could see his mother's head bent over her typewriter. There was no way he could enter the hall without her seeing him.

'Let's hang about a bit. Assembly will be over soon. We can see the head then.'

'Someone's seen us. They're coming out.' The someone was his mother.

'What do you want, Alan?' Her eyes flickered over Kathy without actually resting on her.

'Message for Mrs Rutherford from SCAND.'

'Do you want to see her or do you want me to give it to her?'

Alan hesitated. He could hear hymn-singing from the hall; lots of children's heads were turned watching him while they continued to sing mindlessly.

'Will she be long in assembly?'

'About ten minutes.'

Alan realised that most of the children had their eyes on Kathy, not on him. She waved, causing a ripple of unrest. 'Let's leave a message, if this kind lady will pass it on for us.' Her voice was slightly sarcastic.

'This kind lady is Alan's mother.' Angie's tone was dry. 'You haven't introduced me to your friend yet, Alan.'

'This is Kathy Wilson, Mum.' Kathy's face had gone bright red.

'Hullo, Kathy. Nice to meet you at last. Well, what is this mysterious message?'

'When the children come back this afternoon, could they be organised to sit down in rows in the road. Pam Webb wants the convoy to meet a solid sea of kids.'

'I hope the lorries stop in time.' Kathy smiled feebly at Angie's joke. 'All right, I'll tell Mrs Rutherford all that before the assembly ends, so that she can brief the children. You can come in with me if you like—'

'I'm sorry I was snide,' burst out Kathy, 'but you were glaring at Alan, and I didn't realise you were his mother.'

'Mums do tend to glare, don't they?'

'Er. . . .' Again Kathy blushed. 'I mean. . . .'

Angie laughed. 'I did eye Alan with great suspicion, I agree. I thought he must be playing truant. I'd forgotten he wasn't at school this week. Relax, I'll make sure the kids arrive on time — which is when?'

'By two o'clock, when the convoy is supposed to be coming back.'

'Funny they should tell you their timings.'

'They want to keep in with the locals.'

176

'Some hopes.' Kathy smiled at Angie nervously.

'You ought to come yourself this afternoon, Mum. It was a great turnout this morning.'

'I'll be interested to see Ken Pope's St George and the dragon. I got mixed reports from the children. Luke said the dragon was yukky, just an old forage harvester with bits falling off.' Kathy giggled. Angie turned towards her. 'By the way, I hear you were in the papers again, Kathy. I take it you're the Kathy Wilson who let off a stink bomb in the power station?'

This time it was Alan who went red. His mother had no idea yet that he'd been there, too. The whole conversation was getting too near the edge.

'We must go back, Mum. See you later. Come on, Kathy.'

'You should have warned me your mum worked here,' said Kathy as they went out of the gates.

'She doesn't know I was with you at the station on Friday,' said Alan, ignoring her remark.

'Why didn't you tell her?'

'She's friendly with the guy who fixed it up. I thought there might be trouble about the stink bomb.'

'I'll tell her it was absolutely nothing to do with you.'

'She won't believe you.'

'It's true, damn it.'

'She still won't believe you. She thinks the two of us together mean trouble.'

'Mind you, she has a point there.' They both laughed. Alan felt a rush of warmth towards Kathy. All the accumulated irritation had vanished that morning.

'Come back to my place, and we can make ourselves some lunch,' he said, completely forgetting there was nothing to eat.

'I can't really. I ought to pop back to school. If I go now, I'll make it for my French lesson.'

'Aren't you coming this afternoon?'

'Sure thing. I'll just give school a miss. Guy's coming this afternoon, too; he couldn't make it this morning because he had an interview in London.'

Kathy put on her helmet. With her face hidden away, her eyes suddenly looked secretive.

'Alan! Yoohoo!' The Weasel's voice came loud and clear.

'I'm off. I can't stand that girl. See you later.' Kathy made her usual speedy exit from the scene. The Weasel drew up on her bike.

'Wasn't it smashing this morning! I felt so proud to be part of it all!' Her narrow unappealing face was pink with excitement. Her eyes shone, more bulbous than ever. Alan stared at them; they were practically bulging out of their sockets. Poor Weasel; she was one of the few people whose face didn't improve when it was happy. Alan felt very sorry for her, but still found it a pain to be near her.

'And I've just persuaded my parents to lend our caravan for the blockade. They're bringing it up later on. Pam is thrilled.'

'Why the caravan?'

'For people on blockade duty. After all, that's going on night and day.'

'I haven't got my rota yet.'

'I've been helping Pam work them out.' She said this with such satisfaction that he knew it boded ill for him and Nick. She had been pursuing both of them, but especially Nick. Alan shook Elspeth off, and headed for the Popes' farm, partly to warn Nick and partly to beg some lunch off them. But he found no one there, not even Jean. Haggis was asleep on the back step; the chickens pecked round him busily. Except for the whine of the power station, the farm was silent.

Chickens, oddly enough, are very resistant to radiation. No one knows why, but the dangerous dose for them is fifty times higher than for humans. All other living things – people, trees, grass – perish, but chickens are hardly affected. All that happens is that they get aggressive. They even attack rabbits. They actually peck through their skulls, like birds of prey.

From *Sarcophagus*, a play by V. Gubaryev

SEVENTEEN
Monday, 23 June

When he got back to Tanner's Corner, Alan found lots of people still there, including the Popes. Alan went straight to Pam Webb's buffet and persuaded her to give him some sandwiches in return for going to the school. Nick came up.

'Get a load of that,' he said, nodding towards a large well-dressed man who was wandering about smiling and shaking hands, followed by a crowd of press photographers. 'We are being honoured with a visit from William Tyneham, Conservative Member of Parl-i-a-ment for Stagwell and Maldham. Aren't we lucky? So good for morale.'

They watched Tyneham trying to talk to Ollie Tanner; Ollie was more interested in complaining about self-employed tax-levels than matters nuclear.

'It's a bleeding scandal, Schedule D is. . . .' Tyneham couldn't get him off the subject, and managed to escape in Alan and Nick's direction.

179

'Hullo, boys. Nice to see some young people caring about general issues.' As he shook hands with them, Alan could see Nick gritting his teeth.

'I heard you saying that we had nothing to worry about,' began Nick belligerently. 'With a nuclear power station on our doorstep and a dump in the offing, that's a crazy view.'

Tyneham kept his smile in place. 'I was referring to the drilling, in fact. I said let the drilling go ahead, because very likely they will come to a negative conclusion.'

'Then why spend all this money on a pointless test drill?' Alan asked.

'Taxpayer's money at that, yours and mine.' Ken had come up; other people were joining the group, too.

'Because Nirex own the land, and they can do what they like,' said Pam. 'That's right, isn't it? They bought the land off the power station.'

'Ah, now, I'll have to verify that.' Tyneham obviously didn't know that fact. He looked round the circle of suspicious, unresponsive faces. 'But as to Nirex doing what they like — they can't. There are very stringent guidelines. You will not be put in danger, I promise.'

'We're in danger already.' A familiar voice spoke from the edge of the group. Kathy had arrived. 'Forget the proposed dump. We've got two old Magnox reactors sitting a mile away from us. They should be closed down.'

'Now, that's another issue completely,' said Tyneham, cheering up, 'and I feel we shouldn't confuse the two.' A large car was easing its way up to Ollie's garage. He eyed it with relief. 'I'm afraid I can't stay any longer, but it's been most valuable meeting you all. I do appreciate the reasons for your concern, I assure you, and I will make sure your views are properly represented in the right quarters.'

'Rhubarb, rhubarb, rhubarb,' said Alan as the car drove off. 'What a load of flannel.'

'Do you realise about seventy per cent in this area vote for that twit?' said Kathy as she came beside him. 'And I bet he's come down here just because Nirex think he can calm us down.'

'It looked like that, I must say. I've voted Tory all my life, but this business has upset all my opinions.' Pam handed Alan and Nick a cake each. 'Anyone seen Elspeth? She was going to help me hand out the rotas.'

Nick, Alan and Kathy melted rapidly away.

'Nick, the Weasel is out to get you. She'll put you on a night-time rota with her alone, and then ravish you. I could see it in her eyes.'

'No way will I do a stint alone with her. I'd rather die.'

The road filled with row after row of sitting children made national news headlines that evening. When the Nirex convoy arrived, it was confronted by a sea of nervously grinning faces. The children in the front row were very small indeed; one or two started to cry when they saw the vehicles. One little girl got up and ran back through the crowd to find her mother, screaming: 'I don't like them, I don't like them!'

Amidst laughter, the rest of the children started to chant: 'We don't like them! We don't like the dump!' The men in the convoy looked helplessly at the mass of children. Adults were away at the back. To reach any adults the men would have to pick their way through the children. They stood outside their vehicles talking gloomily together.

Then Henry Gordon shouted: 'We'll be back tomorrow. We'll be back every day until we get through.'

'You'll never get through!'

'Never, never, never,' shouted the children. They cheered loudly when the convoy started to back away, and then lots of them got up and ran up the road after it, mocking and jeering.

'Push off!'

'Go back to London!'

Several teachers rushed after them, trying in vain to restrain them. It took some time to get St George's Primary School under control again. Alan noticed that his brother had been a front runner, shouting louder than anyone else.

'Well done,' he said as Luke was marched past.

Luke's face was red with anger. 'Well done nothing. I'm getting a detention for that, my teacher said.'

Alan immediately went up to his mother to protest about this.

'Listen, Alan, it's none of your business, or mine. They were told to sit still, not tear after the convoy yelling like animals. It gave a very bad impression.'

'Kids get excited when they know they're on telly. They oughtn't to be punished. It's not fair.'

'I hope that's the last time we all have to come up here. It's destroyed a whole day.'

Alan rolled his eyes as his mother went off.

'At least she came,' said Kathy. 'I couldn't get mine to move.'

With the departure of the school, everything went flat. The police started clearing people off the road. Rotas were given out to the members of SCAND, and soon the only people at Tanner's Corner were the hard core of supporters and a few members of the press.

When they saw Elspeth bustling about with rotas Alan and Nick went and hid in Ollie's den. They peered out and saw the pink tracksuit with its Mickey

182

Mouse standing next to Kathy. Kathy was arguing over her rota.

'Bet you she hasn't put Kathy with one of us, but with some old fogey.'

Kathy rode off looking furious, and the Weasel was looking around her.

'Duck, quick. She's on the prowl.' They both crouched beneath Ollie's malodorous kitchen table. Rows of unwashed milk-bottles lay under it, some smelling disgusting and some beyond the disgusting stage. The door opened.

'There you are,' said Elspeth. 'I was looking for you.' She gazed in puzzlement at the boys. Alan began collecting up milk-bottles. Nick picked up a few as well, and followed Alan over to the single tap over a small sink in the corner. Both boys groaned inwardly when Elspeth said: 'What a tip this place is. No wonder you've decided to clear it up. Let me give you a hand.'

'No, don't bother. We're only doing a few—'

'Just look at this one. It's got a dead mouse in it.' She held up the bottle.

Ollie Tanner came through the door. The Weasel was rootling under the table for more milk-bottles, her bottom in the air.

'Here's one full of fag ends,' came her muffled voice.

Ollie looked at the boys, looked at her bottom, and looked at the boys again. 'What the bleeding hell's going on, then?'

'Nothing, Ollie. We're just off.' Nick made for the door as Elspeth was straightening up. Alan stood with a bottle in either hand, frozen.

Ollie glared at Elspeth. 'What do you think you're effing well doing here?'

'I thought the boys were clearing up for you,' she quavered.

'I'm fed up with everybody tramping about and interfering and ruining my business. Put those bottles back. I'll clean them up when I feel like it, Miss Busybody.' Ollie was on tiptoe with anger.

'Look, Ollie, it's nothing to do with her—' began Alan.

'Bugger off, the lot of you. This is the only place I can get a bit of peace. Nagging females everywhere. Give me nuclear pollution any day. I've had enough of these do-gooders.' He watched the three of them put back the offending milk-bottles and held open the door for them to leave.

'Sorry about this, Ollie,' muttered Alan. 'I'll tell you the full story one day.'

'Don't think I'm interested, son, because I'm not.' His little bloodshot eyes were distinctly unfriendly. Alan gave up and followed the others. The Weasel was looking tearful.

'Got to rush. I'm late already.' Nick shot away.

'I don't think Nick likes me,' said Elspeth. 'He's always rushing off.'

'He's got a dentist appointment.'

'He's always got those, too. I've never known anyone go to the dentist so much.'

'He's got very bad teeth.'

Alan gazed round in desperation, looking for a good reason to escape. Suddenly Elspeth started smiling happily; she had seen the approach of the Riley caravan.

'Here comes my dad with the caravan.'

'Wonderful. See you around, Elspeth.' Alan leapt on his bike and made for Stagwell Quay. He found Nick pulling the dinghy down to the water. They both jumped in and started to row out as if Elspeth was still pursuing them.

'Milk-bottles,' said Nick at last, breaking the

silence and shipping his oars. 'Milk-bottles.' They
began to laugh. 'Milk-bottles.' They rolled about in
the boat, screeching with laughter. 'Poor Weasel. She
never gave us our rotas, either. Milk-bottles.' Their
laughter echoed round the estuary, through the gulls'
cries, the tinkling of the marker-buoys, and the ever-
present whine.

Kathy rang at ten-thirty that night.

'I'm in Stagwell Village, Alan. Come and help me
put a banner up. I want to hang it on the scaffolding
beside the other one. I'd rather you helped me than
the lot on duty.'

'Who's up there?'

'Two men and Pam.'

'One's probably Jim Webb, then. OK. Give me
five minutes.'

Kathy had a large bundle in a rucksack on her
back. Alan could see sheets of cardboard and some
rope. 'I've spent all evening making this. It's a whole
lot of separate letters hanging from a rope.'

'What does it say?'

'Aha. I think you'll like it, though. Well, not
exactly like it. . . .' Her entire crash helmet seemed
to grin wickedly.

'Tell me.'

'No. Wait till you see it up. The world's press are
going to be at Stagwell tomorrow, and I want to give
them something new to look at.'

'More press than we had today?'

'Publicity breeds more media people.'

'You're obsessed with publicity. They're much
more likely to have gone back to London.'

Kathy took no notice, but started pushing her
moped to Tanner's Corner. When they got to the
blockade site, they found Pam, Jim and a man called

Les Hounslow drinking tea laced with whisky in the Rileys' caravan.

'Hullo, kids. What are you doing here? You're not on the next watch.'

'We'd like to put up another slogan on the scaffolding.' Kathy was at her most charming. 'If that's all right. There's plenty of room. I thought something new for tomorrow might be a good idea.'

'Go ahead. You're a great one for new ideas, aren't you?' Pam smiled a slightly barbed smile. Then a car approached, and her attention was deflected. It only contained a local farmer, but from the way she flagged him down he could have been the entire Nirex convoy in disguise.

'Old cow,' muttered Kathy. 'Come on, help me thread these letters on to the rope. Each one is numbered in order.'

Slowly the words were revealed: NUCLEAR FALLOUT: A SURE CURE FOR AIDS. Alan laughed, shaking his head in mock despair.

'Kathy, you're crazy. I hope Pam doesn't make you take it down when she sees what it actually says.'

'It's too dark to read easily. Anyway, why the hell should she? It's time we had some black humour.'

They climbed the rather unsteady scaffolding towers and stretched the rope across, realigning the letters before they finally tied complicated knots. It looked good. Kathy and Alan tried to get away unnoticed, but Jim Webb stuck his head out as they passed.

'Good night, Jim,' said Alan.

'Hang about. Let's see the results of your labours.' Jim moved forward in the darkness until he could read Kathy's banner. He began to chuckle. Pam and Les came out, too, and though Pam tried to join in the general appreciation she obviously disapproved.

'I hope that won't start the general public thinking that Stagwell is a gay stronghold.' Withering looks from the teenagers made her gabble on: 'Of course it's true in a way. That slogan, I mean. But sick, though.'

'It'll catch the public eye for sure,' said Jim, 'and that's what a slogan's about.'

'No one will deny Kathy's good at that,' said Pam. Kathy dragged Alan away.

'I could murder that woman. She certainly doesn't like me.'

'Women don't seem to.'

'Seem to what?'

'Like you.'

'I think that's unfair.'

'Men like you.'

'Nick doesn't.'

'He does. He's just annoyed with me for giving you too much time and attention.'

'I don't know what he's worrying about. There's nothing between us.'

They were out of sight of Tanner's Corner, at the verge where Kathy had left her moped.

'I think there is.' Alan stopped. He took hold of Kathy's arms. He wanted to kiss her, but was nervous of making a mess of it. He hadn't exactly had much practice, and he was sure Kathy had. She looked at him with an odd expression in her eyes. Her arms remained completely relaxed, though Alan's grip was tense. He let her go.

'I wish I was older.'

'That's not important.' They remained staring at each other, eye to eye. 'I really like you, Alan. I like you better than anyone else at school. You're a real friend. I trust you, which is more than I can say of *anyone* else.' She put a hand up and touched his

187

cheek. 'But I don't feel there's any more than that between us. Not on my side. And if there is on yours — forget it. I'm not worth it. I'll only hurt you.'

Alan stared blankly into the dark vegetation around them. 'Is there anyone else?' he said at last.

Her eyes did not move, her face did not change. She swallowed. 'No,' she said.

They both knew she was lying.

EIGHTEEN
Tuesday, 24 June

'Listen.' Maddy's breakfast tea steamed as she sat on the backdoor step, cradling the mug and turning her face up to the sun.

'Move up.' Alan brought his mug over and sat beside her. 'Can't hear anything.'

'That's the point.'

'*I can't hear anything*. My God. There's no whine. What's happened?'

'Perhaps they've been persuaded by all the protest yesterday, and turned the reactors off for ever.'

'You've got to be joking.'

'I was.'

'But why the silence?'

189

'I thought you'd be over the moon about it.'

Alan drank his tea, his eyes shut. The absence of the whine was like his sense of emptiness over Kathy. After a while he said: 'Of course I am. But it worries me, too. It could just be shut for maintenance. Or perhaps they've discovered a huge fault.'

The phone rang.

'The silence is golden,' said Nick.

'I know, but why have they shut the reactors down?'

'Dad rang the station, and they said it was for routine maintenance.'

'If it was routine, why didn't they tell me last Friday it was going to happen? I asked a question directly about that.'

'Search me. But I'll tell you a strange thing,' Nick went on. 'The power station looks a lot bigger and more threatening silent. It's made me realise how awful it's going to look when all that's left is a great concrete tomb.'

'It doesn't bear thinking about.' While Nick talked, Alan watched his sister, sitting in the sun with her short hair like a neat wiry halo against the light. She was throwing bits of gravel aimlessly. The clacking of the gravel hitting the path was the only sound audible, except for a fly buzzing round the breakfast-table.

'I'm going up to Tanner's Corner,' said Nick. 'Apparently Nirex have already tried once and been turned back, and they're coming again today but haven't said when. And the police are beginning to get stroppy.'

'See you up there.'

Alan made some toast, and stepped over his sister to eat it in the garden. They both had the week off from school because there were still some exams going on.

190

'Bliss.' Maddy stretched. 'I'm going to sunbathe all day, and read a sloppy book, and give myself a full manicure if I've got the energy. Bliss. What are you going to do?'

'Up to Tanner's Corner. There should be some action there today.'

'Wasn't it good on the box last night? Everyone's heard of Stagwell suddenly, instead of not knowing we even existed.'

As Alan was leaving, he saw Elaine Norrington in the street. She waved to him.

'What do you think of the silence?' she shouted. 'Isn't it wonderful?'

'Wonderful, but why has it happened?'

Elaine came over to the pavement on Alan's side. 'The official story is maintenance. My theory's different. I think they've got a nasty attack of corrosion. Paul denies it, but I know when he's lying.'

'Corrosion?'

'There's been corrosion of important bolts and standpipes in Magnox reactors for ages.' She smiled at him, oddly eager to talk. 'They keep trying to halt it.'

'What effect could this corrosion have?'

'Well, of course I haven't been given any precise facts, but I know that the fuel rods could become wedged and not function properly. They would shut down the reactors at once if there was any danger of that. They've got another problem, however. More serious. Don't quote me, but I've heard that oxidisation is affecting important bolts which hold up the graphite core of the reactor. If those bolts collapsed, the operators wouldn't be able to insert the control rods and, if they can't do that, they can't shut down the reactor.'

'But it *is* shut down.'

191

'Quite. So it's either because they fear the latter might happen, or the former, or both. Or, as they have said, it's routine maintenance.'

Alan stared at Elaine Norrington. 'How on earth do you manage to put up with the nuclear bit if you're so against it?'

She turned her head away. 'It's crept up on me, Alan. When I married Paul, he was a technician in an ordinary power station. You can't predict the route your life is going to take. Here I am married to a committed pro-nuclear station manager. Yet given the chance I'd be up at Tanner's Corner with the rest of you. By the way, I enjoyed "Radiation Stinks"—'

'That was my friend Kathy's idea—'

'Paul was hopping mad.' She got her car keys out. 'Ah, well, I must go. Did your mother tell you we were leaving Stagwell soon? No? I expect she forgot. Paul's been given promotion; we're off to Dungeness where he'll be manager. Up the nuclear ladder we go. Hey ho.'

Alan watched her drive away; she was a bit mad, he thought, but nice. What a life she had. Perhaps she'd break out one day and rush screaming round Paul's next power station with a hatchet. Anyway, he was glad they'd soon be gone.

He bicycled up to Tanner's Corner and was amazed at the crowd he found there. Instead of the few people on duty he expected, there were hundreds. The media were everywhere: all the national newspapers and television networks who hadn't covered Stagwell the day before were down in force. It was bedlam. He saw Nick over by the Riley caravan, from which Pam's face stuck out. She was shouting at Guy, who was struggling with a table.

'No, not on the road. The police are very touchy today. Bring it here.'

192

Guy pushed his way through the crowd and set his table up near the caravan. He grinned at Alan.

'Those boxes have got dozens of printed T-shirts in them.' Guy pointed to some boxes by his car. 'If you could help me bring them over, we can get going.'

'Help Guy, would you, Alan?' shouted Pam at him simultaneously.

'What do you think I'm doing?'

'Sorry, love. There's so much going on. . . .'

Alan followed Guy through the crowd to his car, which was parked at a severe angle on the verge. As they picked up the boxes, Guy nodded towards Kathy's new banner, which in the light of day was larger and clearer than any other. It was attracting a certain amount of attention.

'Who was responsible for that?'

The fact that Guy had been told nothing by Kathy cheered Alan up considerably. 'Kathy Wilson and I put it up last night.'

'NUCLEAR FALLOUT: A SURE CURE FOR AIDS. You have to laugh. I take it Kathy thought of that. She is a bombshell, that girl. She kept the balloon party greatly amused, I can tell you. My father took a tremendous shine to her.'

Guy had loaded Alan with boxes, leaving himself very little to carry.

'How did you like her yourself?' Alan kept his eyes down on his load, and his voice light.

'OK. A change from the girls I usually go about with, to put it mildly.' He winked at Alan, and led the way back to the caravan. Alan decided Guy was an Irredeemable Sloane after all. Kathy couldn't have had anything in common with him. This thought should have reassured him, but it didn't.

Sir Oliver Winter came up, frowning. 'Whoever put up that banner? I think it's in very poor taste.

I'm sorry SCAND have descended to cheap effects like that.'

'Oh, come on, Father. It's caught the public eye already. And any publicity is good publicity.'

'I'm not sure I agree with that.'

Guy ignored his father, who went off to complain to Ken Pope. Guy and Alan started to lay out the T-shirts; they were in various colours, with *Stagwell Says No* on the front. Elspeth came up, offering help. Guy gave her the price-list, and told her to be on the till. He then began to shout: 'Roll up! Roll up! Buy your protest T-shirt! Reasonable prices! Roll up! Roll up! Come on, madam, I'm sure you could do with another T-shirt, and the money's all in a good cause.' Guy's patter was endless; he sold T-shirts steadily all morning. Elspeth gazed at him with adoring eyes as she handled the change.

'Look at that,' muttered Nick to Alan. 'We could be saved. She's obviously switched her interest to Guy.'

The morning passed pleasantly for everyone. People chatted in the sunshine, enjoying the absence of whine; the press circulated, interviewing the locals while they waited for the next bit of action. Endless ice-creams, sandwiches and hotdogs were eaten. At about midday, Alan saw Kathy's helmet bobbing through the crowd. He waved, but she had stopped at Guy's table.

'Come on, Kathy, buy a T-shirt.'

'Can't afford one.'

'Only three quid to you.'

'I haven't got fifty pence, let alone three quid.'

Guy's father overheard this, and insisted on buying Kathy a T-shirt. She did her best to stop him, but he chose her a red one and pressed it upon her.

'This is dead embarrassing,' she said to Alan and

Nick when she finally reached them — they were sitting on a log in the corner of the forecourt with Jim Webb. 'I don't want this. It's got awful sleeves. I'd only wear it if I cut the sleeves off.'

'Cut them off, then,' said Alan. 'Skipped school?'

'I've got a free each side of the lunch break.'

'Need some scissors?' Jim had produced a penknife with a scissors attachment.

'I don't think I dare. . . .'

'Why not? Wearing the slogan's the important thing.' Jim handed her the scissors. She grinned, and laid the T-shirt flat on the tarmac. She took the sleeves off neatly, and cut away at the neck as well. The T-shirt was now a vest, and she put it over the shirt she was wearing.

She handed back the scissors to Jim, who had been watching with interest. He smiled at her. 'I wouldn't say it was an improvement, but each to his own or her own taste.' He got up and wandered off.

'I used to think Jim was wet,' said Alan, 'right under Pam's thumb, a real yesman. But he's not at all. He doesn't take a blind bit of notice of her or anyone. He's great.'

They all stared with liking at the back of Jim's stubbly head.

'His hair looks like he cuts it himself with those scissors,' said Kathy, and in fact she was right.

Suddenly the lazing, chatting crowd was galvanised by shouts from a vantage-point up the road. People rushed into the road and lay down; St George and the dragon were pushed into position. The convoy halted. For a full minute no one moved or spoke. The silence, augmented by the absence of the usual power station whine, was eerie. Then a car coming from the other direction hooted as it nosed through the crowd. It stopped, and out of it stepped the power station manager, Mr Rougemont, with his deputy Paul Norrington. Smiling forcedly, the two men made their way through the crowd towards the convoy, amid shouts of 'What's gone wrong down at the station?' 'Someone dropped a spanner in the works down there?' 'Why the shutdown?'

'Routine maintenance,' the men repeated. 'Nothing to worry about. Routine maintenance.'

Mr Gordon, who had appeared with the convoy on its first visit, was obviously expecting the two men from the power station. They asked to see the SCAND committee. Ken, Pam, Jim and Mark Ableman came forward. Nick, Alan and Kathy edged as close as they could.

'We are still hoping there will be a speedy and peaceful end to this disruption,' began Mr Gordon.

'No problem,' said Ken. 'You take your convoy away permanently, and it will all be over. Speedy and peaceful.' There was some laughter, and a voice shouted: 'Right on, Ken.'

'Unfortunately we can't. We are contracted by the Government of this country to carry out a preliminary survey. That's all it is, a preliminary survey, and we must do it. We have a contract to honour.'

'Let them get on with it.' The voice belonged to a local farmer. 'Let them start the drilling. We've made our point. They'll only discover the land is unsuitable.'

There was a lot of shouting in reply to this. Gordon, Rougemont and Norrington tried to persuade individual members of the crowd that this was a sensible suggestion, but got nowhere. Alan wondered whether the local farmer was a plant of theirs. He certainly hadn't shown his face before.

At last Henry Gordon called for silence. 'We have to warn you all that if you continue to deny us access we will have to consider a High Court injunction. And in addition the police will have to arrest those who refuse to move off the road.'

'We're ready for that,' said Mark Ableman. 'We've taken legal advice, and we've started a fund for any fines we may incur.'

There was so much cheering at this that the pro-nuclear party obviously decided against any further dialogue. Henry Gordon went off with Rougemont and Paul Norrington; someone called out to him: 'Enjoy our beautiful estuary. You'll find it nice and quiet down there today.'

The crowd hooted and catcalled with delight. Kathy turned and muttered to Alan: 'Everyone's behaving like children. It would be much better to take a tough line with them. They think that at heart we're not serious.' She pulled out from the body of the crowd; Alan followed her. He could see her point, though he'd enjoyed shouting with the rest of them.

'I've got to get back to school. I've got a French lesson in half an hour. Where's Guy?'

'On the other side of the road, near the dragon.'

Kathy stared across at him, frowning. 'I can't be bothered to fight my way over.'

'Do you want me to give him a message?' Alan didn't want there to be a message but, if there was one, he'd have liked to know what it was. Kathy took no notice, but started her moped and nosed it past the convoy, which hadn't backed away yet. One of the drivers leant out and wolf-whistled at her. Kathy gave him two fingers.

THE BEST ENERGY SOURCE
Without sufficient energy the world will become a
cold, hungry, economically depressed place, with
countries competing ruthlessly for dwindling supplies
of fossil fuel. These risks are surely worse than those
of well-controlled nuclear risks.

United Kingdom Atomic Energy Authority

NINETEEN
Tuesday, 1 July

The Nirex convoy returned at unannounced times,
but was always successfully stopped by the blockade.
The night rota was discontinued when it was realised
that there was a law limiting Nirex to operations
between 7 a.m. and 7 p.m. only. Plenty of people
manned the blockade during the day, and it was clear
that the contractors were getting very frustrated at their
lack of access. Tempers ran high at every encounter.

On Monday, 30 June the convoy didn't turn up;
Nick and Alan had a very boring two-hour stint
before going back to their work on the farm. (Ken
was employing both boys, since there was no need
for them to return to school until the next term. Those
who wanted to opt out of the last few weeks of the
summer term and take a job had been given permission to do so.)

The boys started their working day very early,
and it was about half-past six when Alan set off the
following morning. He always took the flat route to

the Quay now, because it took him past the entrance lane to Saxon's Field and he liked to keep an eye on it. This particular morning there was a fine misty drizzle falling, and as he went past he hardly looked down into the Field. But his eye registered movements, and he heard shouts. He went back to the lane and rode a few yards down it until his view was clear.

He saw the familiar convoy parked in the middle of Saxon's Field. Men were going in and out of the warehouses at the far end; there were two extra lorries already unloading gear. Alan stood in horror. The whole convoy had arrived during the night. They'd beaten the blockade. They'd got round the limitation law by simply ignoring it.

Alan flew down to the Popes' farm and rushed into the kitchen where Ken, Jean, Nick and Michelle were just finishing their breakfast. The air was heavy with fried bacon and hot toast.

'Have some toast, Alan,' began Jean.

'Nirex have got into Saxon's Field. The whole convoy plus reinforcements.'

'You're joking.'

'I've just seen them.'

'Bloody hell.' Ken went straight to the phone and got through to Robin Hawkes. 'They're in. The whole lot are in Saxon's Field. Yes. OK. I'll go up there now. You ring the Webbs.' Ken drank off a mug of tea in one swallow. 'Come on, boys. Robin's called an emergency meeting for tonight, but in the meantime let's use our initiative. Off we go.'

'Finish your breakfast, Ken, do.' But Ken walked out of the door; if he heard, he took no notice. Jean handed Alan his untouched slice of toast and marmalade. The three of them jumped into Ken's old truck and set off so fast Ken nearly missed a corner.

'Don't kill us all, Dad. A few minutes won't make any difference.'

When they reached Saxon's Field, they found Jim Webb already there.

'The buggers are in,' he said in fury. 'The buggers are in. I was just leaving to do the seven o'clock stint up at Tanner's Corner, when Robin rang me. I couldn't believe it.'

'We'll have to start blockading down here,' said Ken. 'And damn the consequences.'

They stood staring at the drilling rigs mounted on their transporters and the men hurrying about looking smugly busy and pointedly ignoring the forlorn group at the gates. Equipment was being unloaded and stored in the warehouses. Behind them, against the skyline and the estuary, stood the silent bulk of the power station, its edges furred in the drizzle.

'Two rigs. They are planning to bring in five. We'll stop them. We'll have to get back to a night rota again.' Ken raged up and down.

'The trouble is,' said Jim lugubriously, 'they'll win in the end. Despite all our efforts, they're bound to.'

'We'll give them a rough run, that's what. If you're giving up, Jim Webb, don't stand around spreading gloom. Go off and drive your taxi.'

'I'm not giving up. I'm just being realistic.' Jim looked hurt.

'There's a car coming!' shouted Nick. Everyone promptly lay down in the lane, across the gateway. Henry Gordon drove slowly up, and when he saw them raised his eyes to heaven in genuine dismay.

'You realise you're on private property and we could prosecute you for trespass.'

'Yes, we do. Go ahead. Like we said, we've got a fund to cope with fines.' Ken sat in the mud with his gumboots stuck awkwardly out in front of him.

Alan could feel wet mud oozing through his jeans.'

'Will you just allow me to go past and see my men?'

'Feel free. But you'll have to walk. The car's not going in.'

As Henry Gordon stepped from the car, everyone stared at his thin city shoes. The earth all round, wet from the night's drizzle, was nicely churned up by the lorries. He started to pick his way carefully through the mud, but within a few yards realised it was impossible to keep his feet dry. He took off his shoes and socks, rolled up his smart trousers, and set off again, his thin white legs making him look oddly like a bird.

'Poor bastard,' said Jim. 'Don't suppose he'll do that again in a hurry.'

'Right, everyone stand up for the moment, but be ready to sit down again at any sign of trouble.'

Soon they were joined by lots of other people, as word got about that the convoy was in. Some came to help, and others just to stare. Power station workers driving past tended to smile as they slowed down. Ron Dews was grinning widely.

'I could smash his face in,' said Nick, who happened to be out in the road with Alan when Dews went past. 'Just as well Dad didn't see him.'

The Weasel came panting up the road. She was on the point of tearing her hair when she saw the contents of the field.

'It's worse than I thought,' she wailed. 'I always said we shouldn't have given up the night rota. Oh, boys, isn't this awful?' She rushed on down the entrance lane to join the group at the gates.

'It's funny how she kills everything stone dead,' said Nick, 'yet when somebody like Kathy says exactly the same thing we don't mind at all. Come on, let's go home. I need a break.' They started to walk briskly down the road to the Quay.

'You used to mind what Kathy said.'

'Not any more. Anyway, I like her now. She's the most interesting girl around, without a doubt.'

Alan was so pleased by Nick's words that he missed his next remark.

'What was that?'

'I said I wouldn't have thought Guy Winter was her type at all.'

'Why do you think he's her type?' The warmth he had been feeling died completely.

'She was at the cinema with him the other night. Rumour has it she was all over him.'

'Who told you that?'

'Chris. Or was it Barney? One of them happened to be sitting not far behind them. Then she drove off with Guy in his Golf. For Kathy Wilson to give up her moped things must be serious.'

Alan said nothing. He was heartsick; not only had what he'd feared come about, but from the light way Nick was talking he hadn't regarded Alan's involvement with Kathy as anything important. He trudged along in silence, his whole wet, cold, muddy being merging with the grey rain-laden skies.

Nick and Alan dried themselves out by leaning against the Aga, while Jean fed them with hot soup.

'So they're well and truly into Saxon's Field.'

'Dad wants to stop the last three drilling rigs getting in.'

'He won't succeed, but he'll have fun trying,' said Jean drily. 'He's really enjoyed himself the last few weeks. I haven't seen him so cheerful since he took on the Council over that sewage outlet.' She was sitting at the kitchen table, gluing together various

202

items of crockery which had fallen foul of the Popes' slate kitchen floor. 'Does your family break so much china, Alan? I seem to do this every month.'

'Mum just chucks it out.'

Jean pursed her lips as she Sellotaped a cup and put it to set.

Nick nudged Alan. 'Let's go and get cracking on clearing the barn.'

'Hadn't you better wait till Ken gets back?'

'We can get a start on it. I don't want to lose a whole day's pay.' Nick dragged Alan out. As they crossed the yard, he said: 'I've had a great idea. Mum's glue got me thinking. Why don't we creep into that field tonight and Superglue every lock we can find?'

Nick gazed at Alan, and Alan stared back, a smile spreading over his face. Then Nick gave a wild whoop, rushed into the barn and started tossing any old bit of rubbish he could find into the air. Alan joined him, throwing stuff about in a wild frenzy, and feeling a lot better when he'd finished. He and Nick lay panting on some bales of hay and quickly planned exactly what they would do.

THE TOMB OF VALERIY HODIEMCHUK

Before going on night duty, Hodiemchuk told his
family they would go that weekend to the next village,
to help his mother plant potatoes. Hodiemchuk's
wife and small son did travel on a bus to the village
just as planned. The little boy thought his father
was still on duty at the plant. And so he was. But
the bus was in an evacuation convoy, fleeing the
radiation of Chernobyl. And Hodiemchuk would never
be able to leave his duty at the plant. His body was
to be covered in cement and abandoned inside. The
huge concrete sarcophagus being built over the
No. 4 reactor will make an awesome tombstone for
his son to visit: as it will, too, for his own children
and his children's children in turn − on through the
many centuries it will take for Hodiemchuk's grave to
become safe.

From *The Worst Accident in the World*

TWENTY
Wednesday, 2 July

'Alan! *Alan!* Are you deaf or something?' Maddy's
head stuck round the door. 'Phone.'

'I was asleep. Who is it?'

'Kathy Wilson.' Maddy's head disappeared.

'Wait! Tell her I'm out.'

Back came Maddy's head. 'I can't now. She'll smell
a rat.'

'Who cares? Tell her I'm asleep, then. Tell her

anything you like. I don't want to speak to Kathy Wilson.'

'Well, well, this is a big change—'

'And I don't want to talk about it.'

Maddy stared at Alan for a moment. He shut his eyes and heard her run downstairs. He lay there, trying unsuccessfully not to think about Kathy. During the day it had been easy; he'd worked so hard clearing the barn that he'd put her out of his mind. But now his imagination was filled with stills of Kathy and Guy together; they seemed to leap out of his subconscious as if they'd been penned up all day waiting. He kept telling himself he didn't care, and tried to remember the worst side of Kathy — the irritating scene in the power station control room, her coldness at Tanner's Corner the other night, her brusqueness and arrogance, her obsessive enthusiasms. None of this worked; all he could think of was the fun he'd had with her, the moments when her lively green eyes were concentrated solely on him. Being tested in the coach on the way to London; standing close to her on the Embankment surrounded by a sea of foreign tourists; climbing the Boadicea monument; talking endlessly over cups of coffee; short but somehow intimate meetings in the school corridors. . . .

Maddy tapped on the door and came in with two mugs of coffee. 'Thought you'd like one.'

'Thanks.'

'I've got a holiday job in Baxter's shoe shop.'

'Great.'

'It's not good pay, but at least it's something.'

'How much?'

'One pound sixty an hour.'

'Slave labour. Ken pays me two-fifty.'

'Farming's harder work.'

'You can say that again. I'm knackered.' Alan sat up and sipped his coffee. He noticed it was ten o'clock; he and Nick had arranged to meet at midnight. Maddy wandered about his room, chatting about this and that. He knew she was trying to take his mind off Kathy.

'I had a nice little nightmare last night,' Maddy was saying. 'I dreamt that when they restarted Stagwell power station it exploded.'

'They won't restart if there's any danger. I believed them when they said they never took operational risks.' Alan yawned.

'Do you think there's a chance they might never start it again?'

'No idea.' Alan yawned a second time. How to stay awake until midnight was a problem.

'I'm going to bed. All this Nuke Puke is exhausting.'

' 'Night, Maddy.'

Alan decided at about eleven he'd go down and pick Nick up at the farm. If he stayed any longer in his warm dry room, he'd fall asleep for the rest of the night. He met Nick on the main road; he was on his way up to Alan's because he, too, was afraid of falling asleep. They went to the lane leading to the entrance to Saxon's Field, having left their bikes out of sight on the main road.

'I've got two tubes each of Superglue. Do you think that'll be enough?'

'Plenty. Careful you don't glue yourself up as well. It's lethal stuff.'

There was no one on duty at the entrance to Saxon's Field; SCAND had decided to keep its blockade up at Tanner's Corner to avoid being arrested for trespass, and Nirex didn't appear to have a guard, though there was a light on in one of the sheds.

'You do all the vehicle doors,' whispered Nick. 'I'll do the padlocks on the warehouses.' They separated, and as quickly as possible squeezed Superglue into every lock they could find. It was wet and squelchy under foot — Alan slipped in the mud and lost one tube of glue in the sticky morass. Nick joined him as he squeezed the last of his second tube into a lorry cab's door-lock.

'Come on,' whispered Nick. 'There's a chap in that shed and he's opened the door.'

'Got any more glue? I've still got that lock to do—'

'Leave it. Let's go. They're going to have a hell of a job as it is getting themselves sorted out in the morning.'

'Wish I'd worn my wellies. My shoes are full of mud.'

They crept through the squidgy mud as quickly as they could. Nick slipped over as well, and both boys started to laugh at the state of each other. Nick picked up a chunk of wet earth and threw it at Alan, who retaliated; by the time they reached the main road, they were covered from head to foot in mud, and helpless with laughter.

'I'm going to have to undress outside the house.' Alan swung his bike into the road. There was a rumble of thunder, and heavy rain began to fall.

'This could wash most of it off before we even reach home,' said Nick. They saw sheet lightning over the estuary, dramatically illuminating both promontories. Thunder crashed overhead. They leant against their bikes and watched the storm.

'I'm glad we've got rubber soles and rubber tyres,' began Alan, when a car came fast round the nearest corner.

207

'Christ! Look out!'

There was an appalling screech of brakes as it hit the two boys. In the split second before he lost consciousness, Alan saw the anguished face of Gerry Steadman beneath him as he sailed over the bonnet of the car.

The release of atom power has changed everything
except our way of thinking.

ALBERT EINSTEIN,

TWENTY-ONE

Click, click, click. Soft rustling. Click, click, click.
It was soothing and mysterious. When at last Alan
opened his eyes in the harsh hospital light, he saw
Angie on a chair beside him, knitting. She was
concentrating on some wrong stitch, and did not
realise he was awake. He wanted to speak, but instead
could feel his eyes closing as if they were doors
protecting him from the outside world. In relief that
his mother was there, he slipped back into his drugged
sleep.

When he woke again, it was dark in the ward.
Lights were on in the corridor outside, and nurses
passed up and down. Things rattled and clattered.
A red light started flashing, and a nurse ran by. A
police siren wailed in the street; someone in the
next bed groaned and coughed. Alan looked all
round for his mother, but there was no one in the
ward except five sleeping figures. He felt a piercing
disappointment. He could see a clock, and the time
shown was eleven-thirty. She'd be at home in bed.
He wished he had managed to speak to her when he'd
woken the first time; then she might have stayed
with him. He ached all over. Tears of weakness
pricked his eyes.

His nose itched; he started to move his hand up to scratch it, and pains shot through his shoulders. His legs felt strange. They felt as if a huge weight was pressing down on them, hurting them. He expected to see a great square weight like the ones that descended in cartoons to squash a character flat, but there was nothing on his legs except a mound of bedding.

Gerry Steadman. Alan saw his face of startled anguish and remembered. He'd been hit. He'd shot up the bonnet of Gerry's car. And Nick? What had happened to Nick? Was he here in hospital? Alan turned his head fretfully, but couldn't distinguish anyone's face in the dark. Perhaps Nick was dead. . . . . Now Alan could hear a terrible crunching of bicycles, and a yell from Nick, cut off as Alan lost consciousness. If Nick had been able to shout like that, perhaps he was all right.

Alan tried to call Nick's name, but his throat was so dry that his membranes felt as if they were stiffening and cracking. He longed for a nurse, but none had passed since the red light went on.

What had happened to Nick . . .? He shut his eyes, aware that a few more tears were collecting. He felt so weak. Glue . . . glue. They'd been gluing the locks in Saxon's Field. What a crazy thing to do. The sort of thing Kathy would think up. Kathy . . . Kathy. He opened his eyes again. Kathy's footsteps were going by; there was Kathy dressed as a nurse. . . .

'Kathy!' Alan croaked. The dark-haired nurse turned into the ward.

'Hullo, you've come round. How's the pain?'

'You're not Kathy.'

'No, I'm Lindy.' The nurse smiled at him. She didn't look a bit like Kathy really. 'Do you need something for your pain?'

'Yes. And I'm thirsty.'

The nurse fetched some tablets, and helped Alan drink a glass of water. He could have asked what his injuries were, but when it came to the point he decided he'd wait until the morning. Knowing wasn't going to change anything. If he was paralysed, he'd rather find out from his mother.

'Of course you're not paralysed! You've got a broken pelvis, a broken collarbone and a broken arm. That's all.'

'*All!*'

'You'll mend quickly. The doctors say you'll be out and about in no time.'

'Mum, what about Nick?' Alan asked this in absolute dread. He had the feeling his mother had avoided the subject.

'He's fine. Didn't anyone tell you? I left a message with a nurse to tell you the moment you came round.'

'I didn't dare ask.'

'Oh, Alan.' She held his hand for a moment. 'Nick was lucky. He was just battered and bruised. He ended up in the hedge — he made a dive for it apparently.'

'I'd been imagining the worst.'

'He's sent you a card. In fact, half Stagwell has sent you something.' Angie drew a box of chocolates out of her bag, and a mass of envelopes.

'The chocolates are from Pam Webb. Shall I open the letters?'

'Go ahead.' Alan shut his eyes as he listened to all the kind get-well-soon messages; again he felt near to tears. It must be something to do with being in hospital, all this wanting to cry.

'I'll stand them up here for you. This is the one

211

I like best. It's the one from Kathy Wilson.'

'Show it to me.'

Kathy had drawn Alan lying in an operating-theatre, with a villainous-looking medical team holding tubes of Superglue. She'd written: 'Hope they stick you together soon!' Alan laughed, but stopped immediately because it hurt so much. Inside the card Kathy had written: 'You and Nick did a terrific job! Nirex were totally immobilised!'

'You're the local hero, Alan. So's Nick. The accident brought the media down in droves, and the gluing made national headlines. Do you want to see the papers?'

'Some time.' Alan felt very detached from the world outside.

'The nurses have got one of the papers with you on the front page; they were talking about you when I came in.'

'When will I see Nick?'

'He wanted to come in today, but Jean kept him at home.'

'He *is* all right, Mum, isn't he? You're not hiding anything from me?'

'He's fine. I'll bring him in tomorrow.'

It was strange, but not until Alan could see Nick for himself, bruises, black eye and all, did he really believe he was alive.

Because Alan was in Maldham General Hospital, he had floods of visitors. Lots of his school friends came, Robin Hawkes came, Kathy came almost every day. Angie brought Maddy and Luke and Nick in every day as well. Sometimes when Alan saw a group of familiar heads approaching the ward he wished they would all turn round and go away. He only wanted to see his family, Nick and Kathy. Having lots of visitors was fine in theory, and bearable in practice if they only stayed a short time, but Alan discovered most people overdid it. Only Kathy seemed to have grasped that five minutes was better than half an hour. And they came in bursting with news of the outside world, and the latest move against the drilling — chaining themselves to the drilling rigs — and Alan couldn't help finding it all remote and unimportant. He wanted his world to stay within the hospital walls. He even began to feel that the protest against nuclear installations was misguided; the nuclear power station was a bit like a hospital, after all. Insulated from the outside world and deceptively safe.

Gerry Steadman walked into the ward one day when Alan happened to be alone, playing patience. At first he didn't recognise Gerry, who was in an open-necked shirt and jeans. Gerry put down a large bunch of grapes and stood hesitantly.

Alan was invaded by a sense of screeching car-brakes, shock, impact and oblivion. His hand started to shake, and he put down his cards in case Steadman noticed.

'I came to say how sorry I am about what happened. It was my fault, I was going too fast, I didn't expect to see anyone on the road. There was no way I could stop in time on that wet slippery surface.' Gerry spoke in a burst, as if he'd been saying it over and over again in his mind, which indeed he had.

'We didn't hear you because of the thunder and rain.'

'It was an awful night.' There was a pause. His hand steady again, Alan began to collect up the cards.

213

'Don't let me stop your patience.'

'It's all right. Find a chair. There are usually a stack of them in the corridor.'

Gerry got one and settled himself down. 'Don't worry, I won't stay long. I know how tiring visitors are.'

'It's OK.'

'How are you feeling?'

'Much better today. They make me move about, which is bloody agony. I'll be home soon at this rate, they say.'

'That's good.' Gerry fidgeted. 'Your mother told me there was no permanent damage. It was the best news I could have. I wish I could have stopped in time. I have nightmares about it.'

'So do I.' There was a pause. Gerry was restless, ill at ease; he bounced his leg up and down. Alan wished he would sit still. 'You know why Nick and I were there in the first place?'

Gerry suddenly grinned at him. 'You didn't half give them all a lot of trouble. Those Nirex guys nearly went berserk trying to deal with your glue.' He chuckled. 'I bet your girlfriend Kathy was part of the plot. It seemed very much her sort of idea.'

'She wasn't, actually.' Alan flicked his cards. He wasn't sure what line Gerry Steadman was taking. After all, he'd been furious about that stink bomb. Absolutely furious. 'It wasn't very clever to let that stink bomb off.'

To his surprise, Gerry laughed. 'Oh, I don't know. It did no harm, as it turned out.' He paused, and his body went still. 'In fact, you could say it did some good.' Alan sensed he was searching for the right words. Beginning to feel tired, Alan shut his eyes and murmured: 'Radiation stinks.'

214

'Exactly. We tend to forget that at Stagwell Mound. We get cocky about it. We get arrogant. We can't understand why people get so frightened. We tell them, and we believe it, that accidents can't happen here. Why can't they accept that? Because it's true — given all the machinery functioning as it should, and human beings behaving as they should, accidents cannot happen.' Alan opened his eyes again. Gerry was looking straight at him, his unease gone. 'Your friend Kathy's stink bomb made some of us stop and think. We began to see Joe Public's point of view a bit better. Particularly because something unexpected happened.' Gerry paused. 'Up to now I've always believed the man who said after the Three Mile Island disaster: "The plants are safe; it's the people who aren't." '

Alan began to wish Gerry would get to the point; he could feel his attention slipping. Gerry leant forward.

'Sorry, are you in pain?'

'A bit.'

'Can I fetch a nurse?'

'No. I'm not due any painkillers yet.'

'I'll go in a moment. I just wanted to tell you how my attitude has changed, so that you could feel your efforts have achieved something at any rate. Yes, that phrase about the plants being safe but not the people who run them. It's lulled us all into a sense of false security. We've got alert well-trained operatives, so nothing can go wrong.'

'Why has the power station been shut down?'

'Because our plant *isn't safe*.' Gerry tapped the table. 'That phrase isn't true any more. At the moment, Stagwell Mound isn't safe.'

'You said it was perfectly safe when you took us round it. Then two days later it was shut down.'

215

Gerry's leg started to twitch again. 'A deep-seated problem suddenly surfaced.'

'What problem?'

'I shouldn't tell you—'

'You owe it to me. You damned near killed me.'

'You remember the model I showed you? How the graphite blocks into which the fuel rods are inserted are contained inside the circular pressure vessel? The blocks are held inside the pressure vessel by important bolts, and some of these have lost sufficient strength through oxidisation. One of them appears to have failed completely, so both reactors were shut down at once.'

Alan shut his eyes again. He was sure he had been told this before, but he couldn't remember who by.

'What happens if the bolts go?'

'The operators can't insert the control rods. Potentially a very unstable situation.'

'So the reactor could blow up?'

'It could.'

Elaine. Elaine Norrington had told him about the oxidisation problem, but he hadn't really believed her.

'What's going to happen now?'

'It's hoped we can cure the problem and restart the reactors within two years.'

'*Restart* the reactors?' Alan's eyes flew open. 'You must be joking.'

'They may be twenty-five years old but they've still got a lot of life in them yet. It would be uneconomic to phase them out now.'

'So nothing's really changed.' Alan stared at Gerry, who was twitching and fidgeting all over the place. 'When you said you'd changed your mind, I thought you were going to tell me you were leaving the nuclear industry.'

'Why should I, Alan? It's my job. I still believe in nuclear power. Until we get a viable alternative, I can't see a way out of it. No, where I've changed is in my attitude to radiation and the public. I feel more open to people's fears. I would never now claim, as I have done in the past, that Chernobyl couldn't happen here. It could, but we will never allow it to happen.' Gerry got up. 'I must go. I've been here too long.' He shook Alan's hand. 'Radiation stinks. We must never forget that.'

'Thanks again for coming to see me.'

'As I said, it's a pleasure. If there's anything I can do to help you don't hesitate to ask. Goodbye, Alan.'

'Thanks for coming.'

'It's a pleasure. I'll keep in touch.'

Alan closed his eyes and drifted off into semi-sleep. Quick footsteps down the ward stopped at his bed. It was Kathy.

'Hey, I've just seen that dreadful man coming out of the hospital. He smiled at me, but I pretended I didn't know him.'

'He's just been to see me.'

'You're kidding.'

'He's OK, Kathy.'

'He nearly bloody killed you.'

'He came to say he was sorry.'

'Big deal.' Kathy's eyes still flashed with anger. She plonked down a paper bag beside the pack of cards.

'Brought you some jelly babies. As well as eating them, I thought we could stick pins in them and pretend they were the drilling team, or Mr Steadman, or whoever.'

'He admitted it was entirely his fault.'

'He probably did it on purpose.'

'Kathy.'

217

'He's going to have to pay quite a whack of compensation. Thousands, Mr Hawkes says—'

'I don't want to think about that yet.'

'Have a jelly baby. What colour do you want?'

'Black.' They chewed in silence for a moment. Then Alan said: 'Gerry Steadman's changed his ideas a bit. He said your little stink bomb escapade made him think.'

'Well, well, well. How truly amazing. And who thought I was being stupid?'

Alan was busy chewing his jelly baby, so he didn't reply. Kathy went on: 'Has Guy been to see you?'

'Not yet.'

'He said he was coming yesterday.'

'He didn't, unless I was asleep.'

'That's why I didn't come myself yesterday. I didn't want to run into him.'

Alan took another jelly baby, a green one this time. He fiddled with it before saying: 'I'd have thought you'd have come together. Everyone says you're crazy about him.'

'That's a lie. Who told you that? It's rubbish.'

'It doesn't matter.'

'Go on, who's been gossiping?'

'Lots of people. You were seen at the cinema with Guy, and going off in his car afterwards.'

'A grope in the Golf is all Guy's after.' Kathy was dismissive. 'In the end I couldn't take the combination of sex and snobbery.'

Alan savoured the words 'in the end' as he ate his jelly baby. 'Guy's never struck me as a snob.'

'You haven't heard him when he's a bit tight. That's enough about Guy.'

They sat in friendly silence for a while. The man in the next bed snored noisily.

'By the way, do you realise SCAND has finally given up trying to stop the drilling? In the last few days Nirex has brought three more drilling rigs into Saxon's Field, and put up all sorts of sheds. Mr Hawkes says we've done our best, and made our point, and there's no more to be done.'

'That was bound to happen in the end.'

'I'm depressed everyone is giving up so easily.'

Alan tried to move, and pain shot through him. Kathy did not notice his hissed intake of breath.

'You and I and the Popes are the only ones prepared to go on doing anything.' Kathy bit the head off a jelly baby with her sharp teeth. Alan could feel his newfound interest in the outside world waning again as the pain took over.

'I've had such a good idea. I wasn't going to tell you yet, but you're so much better today I think I will.' She ate the rest of her red jelly baby. Alan could hear a nurse wheeling the tea-trolley further down the corridor. He longed for a cup of sweet tea.

'The other day I saw this massive padlock in the ships' chandlers in Maldham. It was a mega-padlock, amazing. It gave me a good idea.' Kathy leant forward, having checked to see if anyone was listening. The old man beside Alan was still snoring, and the man in the opposite bed was doing the pools with avid concentration.

'I asked in the shop if they'd lend me a couple of padlocks; I said it was for an amateur production, which is true in a way. No problem.' Kathy's grin was wicked. Alan felt exhilaration warring with pain, and grinned back.

'Well, go on. What are we going to use these mega-locks for, I wonder?'

At that moment the nurse came in with the tea-trolley, and started dishing out cups of weak tea. Alan forgot to ask for sugar. Kathy waited impatiently for her to move on to the next ward.

'To padlock the main gates of Stagwell Mound power station, that's what we're going to use them for.' They gazed at each other. 'We'll publicise it well, otherwise there's no point doing it. We'll pick the time when the shifts change, so that there's a maximum number of people trying to go in and out. We'll have to be very quick, to get all the padlocks on at once, but I'm sure it can be done. Then we'll let them stew for an hour or so.'

'We need to work out all the details really carefully—'

'Give me time. I only saw the mega-locks a couple of days ago.'

'I'm going to be no use; I'll be on crutches.'

'No, in a wheelchair. We need you in a wheelchair. You can sit on the keys in case they try to get them off us by force. And we'll decorate the wheelchair so it looks stunning, and use coloured smoke billowing from it when it's on the move—'

Alan started to laugh, and simultaneously groaned in agony. The ward sister came in when she heard the noise.

'Are you all right, Alan?'

'Fine. It's just that it hurts like hell when I laugh.'

'Don't laugh, then.' She looked sharply at Kathy. 'You mustn't over excite him, you know. He's been badly injured.'

'Sorry.'

'I'll bring you some more painkillers in a minute, Alan. You're almost due your next dose.'

They watched her walk briskly out. Then Kathy leant towards Alan and whispered, her green eyes close: 'I've had another idea as well. Do you think we could get the whole school to march to the power station and stick crosses into the grass outside, hundreds of crosses saying "RIP Nuclear Power" or whatever? Wouldn't it be terrific—?'

'Stop, Kathy, no more. I've had it.'

They heard the ward sister's footsteps returning.

'I'd better go.'

'Come back tomorrow.'

'Of course.'

PLEASE DON'T GO
by Peggy Woodford

It's Mary's first visit to France, and she is enchanted by everything she finds — the place, the way of life, the food, the smells and especially the people. During that unforgettable summer, she meets Antoine — handsome, married Antoine who is more than twice her age and is the first man ever to kiss her. And she also meets Joël — tall, gangly, red-haired Joël who seems to want to be more than a friend . . .

0 552 524573

CORGI

F·R·E·E·W·A·Y

If you would like to receive a Newsletter about our new Children's books, just fill in the coupon below with your name and address (or copy it onto a separate piece of paper if you don't want to spoil your book) and send it to:

The Children's Books Editor
Young Corgi Books
61–63 Uxbridge Road
Ealing
London W5 5SA

Please send me a Children's Newsletter:

Name: ....

Address: ....

....

....

All Children's Books are available at your bookshop or news-agent, or can be ordered from the following address:
Corgi/Bantam Books,
Cash Sales Department,
P.O. Box 11, Falmouth, Cornwall TR10 9EN

Please send a cheque or postal order (no currency) and allow 60p for postage and packing for the first book plus 25p for the second book and 15p for each additional book ordered up to a maximum charge of £1.90 in UK.

B.F.P.O. customers please allow 60p for the first book, 25p for the second book plus 15p per copy for the next 7 books, there-after 9p per book.

Overseas customers, including Eire, please allow £1.25 for postage and packing for the first book, 75p for the second book, and 28p for each subsequent title ordered.